Here
Beneath
Low-Flying
Planes

The

Iowa

Short

Fiction

Award

University of

Iowa Press

Iowa City

Merrill
Feitell

Here
Beneath
Low-Flying
Planes

University of Iowa Press, Iowa City 52242
Printed in the United States of America
http://www.uiowa.edu/uiowapress

The publication of this book was generously supported by the
National Endowment for the Arts.

The University of Iowa Press is a member of Green Press
Initiative and is committed to preserving natural resources.

Printed on acid-free paper

Library of Congress Cataloging-in-Publication Data
Feitell, Merrill, 1971–.
   Here beneath low-flying planes / Merrill Feitell.
         p.   cm.—(The Iowa short fiction award)
      Contents: It couldn't be more beautiful—Here beneath
   low-flying planes—The marrying kind—Bike New York!—
   And then you stand up—The dumpling king—Our little
   lone star—Such a big Mr. England.
      ISBN 0-87745-911-8 (pbk.)
      1. United States—Social life and customs—Fiction.
   I. Title.   II. Series.
   PS3606.E38H47 2004
   813'.6—dc22   2004045979

04   05   06   07   08   P   5   4   3   2   1

For Mom, Dad, and Bennett

Contents

ACKNOWLEDGMENTS

Were it not for the insight, encouragement, expertise,
employment, friendship, and rallying gab of many excellent
people, I never would have been able to finish this project. So
thanks, indeed, are due.

To Brenda Shaughnessy, Joanna Hershon, Kristen Poff, Paul
Bausch, Jill Stoddard, Ellen Umansky, Halle Eaton, Cris Beam,
Robin Goldman, Tom Bissell, Margo Rabb, Tim Carroll, Tayari
Jones, Helen Schulman, Stephen Koch, Michael Cunningham,
Alice and Larry Dark, Tim and Ginny Fitzmaurice, Timothy
Donnelly, Lynn Melnick, Jenny Offill, Angie Cruz, Amanda
Davis, Eleanor Henderson, Ted Thompson, Linne Ha, Scott
Conklin, Mat Johnson, Dan Ehrenhaft, the whole Bausch family,
Carol Houk Smith, Amy Williams, Adam Langer, Jerome
Kramer, George and Caroline Wallace, Batyah Shtrum, Chris
Roebuck, Jamie Mirabella, Ravi Rajakumar, John Wallace,
Deena Luria, Carrie Barnes, Callie Janoff, Chris Kelty, Chris
Francescani, Ed Tonderys, Rick Wormwood, Joe Leff, Karen Poff,
Nate Blakeslee, Henny and Lenny Feitell, Joe Viverito, Anne
Edelstein, Fred Jespersen, Bucky McAllister and Beth Morrow,
Eric and Amy McAllister, Gail Hochman, Marianne Merola,
Joanne Brownstein, and Meg Giles.

To everyone responsible for the education, inspiration, and
bliss that is the Bread Loaf Writers' Conference.

To everyone at the amazing MacDowell Colony, Yaddo, the
Writers' Room, the Bronx Council on the Arts, and the Writing
Division of Columbia University.

To Holly Carver, Charlotte Wright, Sara Sauers, Mary
Russell Curran, Megan Scott, everyone else at the University of
Iowa Press, and, of course, to Matt Klam.

And finally, to Bennett Feitell, my brother and personal
MacGyver, and to Myrna and Larry Feitell, my parents, whose
support has been unflagging and whose hearts and minds are
inspiringly huge.

I can say only this: Thanks. Big.

The following stories, in a somewhat different form, were previously published as follows: "It Couldn't Be More Beautiful" in the *Virginia Quarterly Review*; "Here Beneath Low-Flying Planes" in *Book Magazine*; "Our Little Lone Star" in *Glimmer Train Stories*; "The Marrying Kind" in *Book Magazine*; "Bike New York!" in *Best New American Voices 2000*, selected by Tobias Wolff; and "Such a Big Mr. England" in *Hampton Shorts*.

Here
Beneath
Low-Flying
Planes

It
Couldn't
Be More
Beautiful

It is Thanksgiving, the great day of dinner, of Dockers and dress shirts and marshmallow-sweetened squash. This year we are forgoing our standard slow graze on the home front to spend the day with my sister and her boyfriend's family, meeting them for the first time—on this, a National Holiday. The whole situation has got my parents up in arms. My mother likes to do the cooking herself, and my father has been ranting about the traffic we'll hit the whole way out to Long Island. I know the truth is that my sister is only home from college for the weekend and my parents would rather we have Carly all to ourselves.

"Help me out on this one, Ellie," she instructed me over the phone. "I'm having a hard time getting Mom and Dad to say yes. What you should tell them is that if they don't participate in my life, it's entirely possible they'll get left behind."

So I told them this. I laid it on thick. And now here we are on the L.I.E., making good time and watching the accidents slip past.

"I just hope she's not pregnant," my mother says.

"She's not pregnant," I call out from the very back of our station wagon, where I'm stretched out watching the city recede through the tailgate window.

"Really?" my mother asks.

"Such is my belief," I say. This is something Carly has taught me. She has long advocated the combination of being vague and authoritative. I wait for a response and watch two little girls in an SUV wave to me and press their tongues against the glass. I don't really feel like making faces in return, but I figure I'd better. In an hour or two we might all be stuck together at the same kids' table. I'm fourteen, so I'm never sure where they'll put me.

Carly has been pregnant before—her freshman year. This is something my mother knows but my father does not. She has been pregnant once and had scabies twice, both times from a thrift-store pair of pants, both times Wrangler corduroys. She will declare this kind of thing at a party, and because she is beautiful and skinny and resolute, suddenly it's okay to talk about the pictures of seashores taped to the ceiling of Planned Parenthood, and everyone is anxious to tell their tales of infections contracted by way of thrift-store clothes.

I miss her more than I probably should. She goes to college in Portland, Maine, which isn't so very far but far enough. Besides, she's busy. She wrote a big paper on the socioeconomics of Portland's tattoo parlors and their correlation to the clinical conventions described by Foucault. Her paper was published and it earned her lots of funding. "Funding and a boyfriend," she likes to say. She met Alex at the Painted Lady. They have been going out since July. My parents think it's premature to be getting the families together, but Carly called the shot, I championed the cause, and now it's happening. I talked to her on the phone last night, and she warned me to brace myself for the small talk and the Shelbys' commemorative coin collection.

"We've just spent an entire day discussing the artistry of the Franklin Mint," Carly said. "I'm not exaggerating. It's going to be snooze city for you, Ellie. I'm so sorry, kid."

"Whatever," I said. "I'll bring a magazine."

"Make it a dirty magazine so you can whip it out at dinner and see how everyone responds. One small move and you can keep us both amused."

I thought for a moment about where I might actually be able to find a dirty magazine, but I finally decided I could get Carly rolling with *Business Week*. It's my timing she digs, and the fact that I'm always on her side.

"Answer me this," my father says now. I can hear his sigh all the way from the front seat. "Are these the kind of people who are going to try to make me watch football?"

I don't answer. I never let on a thing. I just watch the city skyline slip away behind us. We come over a rise and the Empire State and the Chrysler Building are there and then gone, ducking out of sight like two sisters with a secret.

We arrive at the Shelbys' at a quarter to three, our father pulling down the long, wooded private road that leads to their house. The house is brown and angular, that old kind of modern, the roof spotted with what seems like too many skylights. There are no shutters or balconies or flourishes, just straight wooden planks and huge windows that come to a peak high among the bald trees. There is a faded croquet set under a bush by the driveway. If it gets boring, I bet Carly and I will come play out here.

My mother opens the tailgate door for me, letting in the cool air, the smell of suburbs, cold grass, and fireplaces. She offers her hand but I slide out on my own.

"Do you need some help with the pears?" she asks. We have brought a tower of foil-wrapped pears as if to offer up something pure to compensate for my sister's blemished past. My mother is always a little apologetic, as if it's her fault that Carly does things like have sex, get pregnant, and write papers on tattoos. She will never bring bottles of wine to these kinds of functions. Just fruit or a book. These pears are arranged on a foam stand spray-painted a refracting silver and gold, which crumbles a little as I slide the thing out.

"All our glory is falling to pieces," I say. There are bits of foil all over the back of the car, catching the light and making rainbows on all the other junk in there—beach towels and magazines, my old flip-flops and Carly's tennis racket. It's like a clubhouse we've abandoned, the disco ball taking one last spin.

Mr. Shelby comes out to greet us. "Welcome! Welcome one and all!" He is not wearing shoes, and his big white feet and their yellowing toes are poking out from his khakis.

"Hello," my mother says. She has bright gray eyes and high round cheek bones which keep her looking young from the front, though in profile you can see how her skin hangs soft and defeated on the sides. She reaches a hand out to Mr. Shelby.

"Come in! Come in!" He booms like he is P. T. Barnum and we are his circus—my mother walking tiny, tightrope steps through the gravel, my father approaching like the strong man with his golden tower of pears, and me crawling out of the tailgate like a clown from an overstuffed car. I hate the Shelbys already.

Mrs. Shelby meets us in the foyer, which has a big mirror in a heavy wood frame, tucked into which are about a hundred family photos. And there I am with my parents, reflected smack in the center. The house smells like things have been cooking for a week solid. Everything is wood, the walls and the floors and the exposed rafters and beams, all of it porous and holding the smell of turkey and apples, baking citrus and celery. I'm sure my mother's having chef-envy. We have not had a normal Thanksgiving in so long. Last year Carly was spending a semester in San Francisco, and we did the whole dinner at the restaurant in the hotel.

"Happy Thanksgiving," says Mrs. Shelby. She has brown spots on her cheek and tissues poking out of her rust-colored sweater sleeve. She is old, which shouldn't surprise me. Alex is eight years older than Carly, who is eight years older than me. It sounds like the start of a logic problem on a standardized test. If we all keep moving at a steady pace, how long will it take to catch up to one another? "This must be Ellie." She smiles at me, hands folded in front of her, tissue catching the thin leather band of her watch.

My mother is standing behind me, her hand resting on my shoulder, guarding my breastbone. I can see it in the mirror pressing where she couldn't if I actually had breasts. She combs a finger lightly through my wimpy hair. I am so plain I can't even look at myself. I am not going to ask for my sister even though I haven't seen her in months. I am not going to scramble after her. I know that if I can hold out, Carly will come to me, but I can't help myself. "Where's Carly?" I ask Mrs. Shelby, and then my sister appears, summoned by my own eagerness, it seems.

She is standing in the archway that connects the foyer to the rest of the bright woodsy house. Her skinny arms are crossed over her stomach so she can scratch at either side of her back. Her hair is dyed a bluish black and the ends are poking out beneath her bony elbows. She's wearing jeans and a cool Indian blouse.

"How's tricks?" she asks me. There's a quiet in her voice no matter what volume she's speaking. It's the register designed for me to understand, a layer of sarcasm, or innuendo, or mockery. I can excavate the meaning without trying. She's telling me it's boring here.

"I'm very excited about my new dress," I say. I bite my lip as I turn in a slow circle, wrists flexed. My dress is a purple and beige plaid sort of pinafore that my mother bought for me to wear over a turtleneck. I'm in loafers and slouching socks. I look like a Catholic-school girl.

"It's lovely. You're a lovely princess," Carly says.

Mrs. Shelby is beaming at us, but my mother knows better. She knows that in this one moment we have managed to make fun of everything in this room, the whole occasion of being here instead of at home, all of us in the kitchen cooking together in shorts and socks.

"Thanks so much for having us," our mother says to Mrs. Shelby. "What a lovely place."

They stand in the foyer talking about the exposed beams and the way the area is booming since the *New York Times* real estate column sent the city people in.

"Come, princess," says my sister. "Let's get Alex and we'll give you the tour."

Carly takes me by the hand and nobody else is invited.

"I brought you something." I stop her in the middle of a sky-lit hallway. I tug her into a bathroom, flip on the light and the fan. Tucked into my skirt pocket are four Popsicle sticks, each one topped with a laminated photo of the members of our family. "If you miss us when you're back at school, you can just have a little puppet show."

I demonstrate holding the Popsicle stick head of my dad and having him say, "Well, well, Carly, answer me this: Must we stay through the whole meal or can we just say hello and then leave?". Then our mother: "You're not pregnant. You promised you'd never get pregnant again—unless it's time. Unless I'm ready."

Carly laughs. She likes weird things, and I try hard to accommodate. She puts her hair up into a bun and pokes our family swizzle sticks into the knot. I can see my puppet face, winking, just behind her ear.

"Thanks," she says. "And thanks for coming."

"Can you explain to me about Mr. Shelby's feet?"

"I believe it's a Depression-era hosting tradition: when there's not enough food, ruin the appetite of the guests."

"I miss you," I say.

"No, you don't," she corrects me. She lifts the earring dangling from my left ear and inspects it. "Did mom get you these?"

I nod.

"Oh." It's unclear if this is an endorsement or a condemnation, but I'm not about to let on that I care enough to ask. "Let's go find Alex," she says. "He's probably giving Dad a lecture on body art and tribal branding." Carly rolls her eyes.

"How fascinating," I say, taking her cue. "He sounds absolutely fascinating."

We find Alex standing with Dad by the living room bookshelves, expounding on the wonders of the tiny Bose speakers set in with all the old hard covers about modern art and war. Alex is skinny and several inches taller than our father; he has to hunch over to look Dad in the eye. He has dark messy hair, but he's wearing a crisp white button-down and spanking new black jeans—what Carly has always called the aging-hipster tuxedo. Under that shirt, I know Alex has Bruce Lee tattooed on one bicep and some hot babe on the other, but now he has his sleeves rolled down, and I wonder for a minute if he's hiding everything from my parents or his own. He nods a lot as he moves books aside, showing my dad some hidden wiring. He's so lanky and quick, he's like a bobblehead doll.

"Hey, Alex," Carly calls softly, but it's like his ears are trained for her voice. He looks up, forgetting my dad and the bookcase and the high-end audio. "This is Ellie."

"I've heard a lot about you," he says, and I believe him. His face cracks into an enormous smile and he starts nodding now in my direction. "What happened to the pink hair? In all the photos you had that pink hair?"

"I got rid of it." My stomach is sort of winding up with something. For the first time I'm nervous that he won't like me. He has a big square chin with a dimple in the middle and I can picture Carly kissing it. I can't stop thinking of myself kissing it. I try to remember certain things Carly has taught me: If you want to be a little scary, she says, speak slowly and look the guy right in the eye. "That's the thing about having pink hair," I tell him. "Even after the fact, all anyone wants to talk about is your pink hair."

"I'm impressed." He gives my parents an amused little smile. "I was practically *eighteen* before I did anything I couldn't seem to put behind me."

Everyone titters, even Mr. Shelby, everyone but me. I'm not sure if Alex is making fun of himself or me, but I don't really have the time to think about it. Mrs. Shelby claps her hands. "Sit. Sit. Everyone sit."

The adults all position themselves on the two plaid couches, which face each other across a coffee table. Just beyond them is a wall of sliding glass doors, two sets looking out to the Shelby's backyard, a hilly stretch of patchy lawn, and then the woods, which have got us surrounded.

Carly and Alex lean together on the bookcase, their long bony bodies side by side. Alex gives my sister's waist a squeeze, and I can suddenly picture him coming with us to the beach, rubbing sunblock under Carly's bikini strings. I don't know if the adults are also imagining Alex and my sister nearly naked together rubbing each other with lotion, but an enormous silence has fallen over the room just at the sight of the two of them standing so close. It's impressive—you can *feel* the secrets surging between them. I can tell my mother is freaking out from the way she keeps recomposing herself, rearranging her hem and her hands in her lap. I smile at Carly and she smiles back. We float up and over the discomfort in the room. It's the first time I've seen my parents act like Carly's life is none of their business.

"So, Ellie," Mrs. Shelby says. "Why don't you tell us a little about you." She leans over her lap toward me to prove she's interested, and suddenly I'm the center of everyone's attention. They want to know what I study, what I like to do after school, and how I feel about growing up in the city. Mrs. Shelby wants to know if I've always been tall or if I had one big growth spurt. Mr. Shelby has a million questions about prep classes for the PSAT. I'm standing at the front of the room, against the glass doors, like I'm in school giving a presentation. Nobody has even offered me a soda. They can ask anything, I realize—I'm a child and I'm theirs. Carly pulls the Popsicle sticks out of her hair and mimics me, bouncing up and down the puppet with my head on it. Mr. Shelby scratches at one foot with the other and asks what they teach in the private schools in eighth-grade bio, like he's trying to figure out if I know about sex yet or not. I would put up with this for no one else but my sister.

Finally, I say, "I think I need Carly to show me the bathroom."

"She's very cute," Mrs. Shelby tells my mother as Carly and I walk down the hall.

"I'll pay you back," Carly promises. "When it's your turn to bring the big boyfriend around."

"You better," I say, though by the time I'm in college, who knows where she'll be?

———

Once we manage our escape, Alex decides to take us on a house tour. He starts by showing Carly and me a picture of himself that's hanging in the hall. It's from his boarding school days when he looked rumpled and naughty, his dark hair a little too long. He looks bigger and broader now, but he's still so thin and he still stands like a boy—with his shoulders hunched and fists in his pocket like he's hiding a handful of dope in there. I can't figure out what it is that makes a person finally look like a certifiable grown-up. He should already. He turned twenty-nine this year.

He shows us a million uninteresting things. He points out a wooden beam in the ceiling that's from an antique whaling boat. He shows us the place on the staircase where as a kid he once got his head caught between the slats. "And this is the kitchen," he says as he pushes a swinging door into the bright and spacious room, where copper pots are simmering on a yellow stove. There is the smell of turkey, wine, and warm bready stuffing. A noise comes from the oven, the drizzle and hiss of fat falling away. On the butcher block there is a set of old wood-handled carving tools, which look worn and exhausted; they almost look like Mrs. Shelby, waiting, tired but patient, for company to come and then leave.

In the past I've had lots of fun hanging out with Carly and her boyfriends. More often than not, it becomes two against one. John Giacometti for example. One summer when Carly was in high school and we had a rental on the Cape, she and I spent a whole Saturday trying to see how many times we could get him to take us to 7–11. "I've forgotten my Chapstick," she'd said. "I'm going to have to go back."

I've forgotten my licorice, my bubblegum, my Geritol. I kept my eye on the odometer; we put on almost thirty miles. He was so whipped on Carly he would have driven to the moon and back without question.

"Listen, Alex," I say. "I don't so much need a tour."

"Well, you're not really getting one." He opens the door next to the brown fridge and it takes me a second to realize it's the garage we're heading for. There is no car and not a lot of stuff around—not like the garages of the summerhouses we've rented. There are no bags of clothes waiting to go to the Salvation Army, no broken skis and wooden tennis rackets, no abandoned easels, or dartboards, or potter's wheels. This garage has been through its final purging. The Shelbys seem to be people who have figured out where to put their past—they've gotten rid of it. Our house is in limbo. We keep everything. Carly's room is still perfectly intact, as if ready and waiting for her to move back home. The one change is that my father set up a fax machine on Carly's desk, and sometimes I'll find him searching for paper clips or scissors lost in her mess. Every surface is covered with rubber spiders and old mannequin parts she found in front of Saks and the slew of chipped teapots she once used for planting aloe. It has never occurred to me until this very second that holding on to all that clutter might just be a phase.

Here in the Shelbys' garage there is just a hose coiled on a hook, a standing fan for the summertime, a washer-dryer setup, and Windex, Fast Orange, and Mr. Clean lined up on a shelf by the window, catching the weak sunlight like liquid stained glass. The concrete floor has been painted a slate gray, perfect and new but for a work-boot footprint right next to the door. The dryer is going, inflicting rhythm on us, pumping humidity and fabric softener out into the room.

Carly hops up onto it, her feet banging against the metal. She sort of undulates her body like she's put a quarter in the thing and is going for a ride. Alex passes her a cigarette, which she passes to me. She pats the washer beside her and I jump up onto it, my loafers louder than I like to be as they bang against the steel. Alex misses a beat, giving Carly a look like he's not about to contribute to the delinquency of a minor.

"It's okay, Chancellor. She can smoke." Carly tugs him by the belt loop of his jeans.

"You smoke a lot?" he asks.

I don't answer. I don't say anything. I just take a light off Carly's match, breathe in, and exhale. Carly always says I'm scariest when I say nothing.

"You were great in there," she says. "Who knew you'd be the front line between me and the third degree." She pinches at the side of my butt; the joke is always that I don't have one. "You've become a fabulous decoy."

I shrug, like it's no big deal, though everyone knows I love making her proud. She wanted a brother or sister for years while our parents kept trying and trying, and I guess she must have absorbed some of their urgency as her own. She has always taken care of me. The story goes that on one of the first cold days I was alive, she wrapped my entire body in yarn to try and make me a sweater. My mother was terrified she'd asphyxiate me.

"So when are you going to come visit us in Portland?" asks Alex.

"Well, when are you going to invite me?"

"You're always invited," he says, like there is an allegiance between himself and Carly that might be bigger than our own.

I press my hip against Carly's and laugh. "I know I'm always invited."

Alex shrugs, like he's too shy to take it, instead of a tattooed guy more than twice my age. Carly doesn't laugh with me. She reaches for him, tugging him by his sleeve until he leans low enough for her to kiss his ear. She pulls him close and leans her head back against his chest as she talks to me, as if this will make him part of the conversation. I can tell by the way he gives in to playing headrest that he probably wants to marry her. Everyone has always wanted to marry her. In high school Carly read to a blind lady who lived in our building, and suddenly everyone at her school was after the Community Service office to find blind ladies who needed to be read to. Watch, if Carly came up with some philosophical thing against tattoos, Alex would probably volunteer to get his own *skin* removed.

He stands to the side of our conversation and starts brushing hair from Carly's neck so he can plant a bunch of little kisses there. I expect her to roll her eyes at this behavior but she doesn't. With one hand, she rubs at Alex's leg, and with the other, she holds her burning cigarette directly toward me. She's like a single star trying to be in two constellations.

"So what's new at home?" she asks me. Her tooth is chipped. I hadn't noticed before and I wonder if my parents know. It's the right one in front, a tiny triangle of it missing, snapped off like a page in a book that's been dog-eared too many times.

"The only big news at home is the DVD player," I say. "One of Dad's students gave it to him and now you can get him to watch anything, as long as you'll watch it in a foreign language. He'll even watch *Pee-Wee's Big Adventure*—as long as you're willing to watch it in French."

The two of them laugh, holding hands.

"Bon Matin, Monsieur Petit Déjeuner," I say, quoting Pee-Wee.

Alex rolls up his sleeves and reveals the veiny insides of his forearms. They are a wash of color, scaly fish, blue and orange. They must be koi, like in Japan. They look like the back of the kimono Carly uses as a bathrobe, and I wonder if that's where Alex got the idea. I get a little nervous watching them—together, watching me. I go on. "And Aunt Carol comes over Friday nights to watch *Iron Chef* with mom. These days everything in the house is dubbed."

I do my Kitchen Stadium routine, and then a little *Star Wars* in Spanish, a little Italian *Cool Hand Luke*. I do every bit I know. I see the two of them laughing together, and it feels no different from performing for the grown-ups in the living room. I'm the one all alone, rattling on and on, their big fat stupid clown. I can't seem to stop myself. "What happened to your tooth?" I ask abruptly. All I want is for her to have to answer to me.

My sister and Alex look at each other and laugh, like they both know what happened, but they're not telling. He kisses the top of her head and I don't get an answer at all.

"So what about you?" Alex asks. He squeezes my sister's hand. "Do you have a boyfriend? If we come visit do we get to meet your special someone?"

"I don't have a boyfriend. I'm *fourteen*."

"Come on," Carly says. "There's no shame to be had about a little sumpin' sumpin'."

I look up at the row of cleaning fluids, looking to the colors and the light for some kind of rescue. I don't know what the right response is. I just wish I could rewind the whole conversation back to the part where Alex asks if I'll come visit. Yes, I would say. Thanks very much. Or if I could roll back time even further, I would take my parents' side that we should have the holiday with Carly, at home, alone.

"What about Kenji? How's Kenji?" Carly prompts. She reaches over to go for my butt again, but I jump away to the floor.

"Kenji is my *friend*," I say. I'm wondering what's going on in the house. I'm wondering exactly how late we'll have to stay here. I start making my way back and forth across the empty garage, pretending I'm walking on the balance beam, umbrella steps, stag leaps, tour jetés. I start talking fast. "Eric Eaton, on the other hand, is a whole other story. Every girl in school loved him—deeply—until field day. He was wearing those shorts with the built-in lining and one of his testicles popped out when he was running hurdles. No one can look at him now. I'm back to my crush on the Rebel Records guy. He never steps out from behind the counter so even if he pops out of his pants, at least I'll never have to see."

Alex stubs his cigarette out on the ground. "Better make sure it's out," I say. "You know your dad's got that thing about shoes."

Alex smiles at me, a long weird smile and I don't look away. It feels like if I can just stare at him hard enough, maybe he'll recognize the might Carly thinks I have inside. Instead he takes my sister's chin, tilts her face toward his, and kisses her. They kiss. I can see his tongue bridging their mouths and I can hear their teeth clack together. I go through the ballet positions doing pliés; I haven't done ballet since I was in the third grade. They're still at it. From the side it looks like Alex is swallowing my sister whole. Her eyes are not open; they are not looking for me. I hate him so much I can't even stand still. I don't know what else to do, so I slip back into the kitchen, where my mother and Mrs. Shelby are peering into the oven.

I sneak by, toward the foyer where we first came in. I grab my mother's long wool coat from the rack and head out the front door.

Outside, it's biting with cold. My legs are bare, pale and flaky; I've forgotten how awful they are in winter. It's not even four o'clock, but the light has gone thin and a little bit green, like the air itself isn't feeling too well. Our car is parked parallel to the house and I walk to the far side of it, making big weird steps to feel my mother's satin lining catching on my goose-bumped skin and the leg hair she still won't let me shave. I sit down on the pebbled driveway, leaning back against the driver's-side hub. I pick up a handful of stones and throw them at the leafless bushes but nothing happens, not even a noise. I feel like such a moron.

There's an odd caw overhead, and I'm not sure why but it starts me crying. I slide down to lie on my back, wrap myself tight in the coat, and imagine falling asleep here, my father finding me stretched out and blocking his door. In my mother's pockets are her standard stash of plastic baggies for picking up after the dog, her keys, and her cell phone, which I turn on and watch glow blue and greet me.

Kenji's mother answers on the first ring, before I can even decide if it's all right to call and intrude on their family dinner. Kenji said they're having quite a crowd. He is my best friend—a boy, but he is not a boy I really like. We just do stupid things and laugh about them. Last week we went up to 101st and Columbus to try buying pot. We stood on the street waving fifty bucks around until a man came over and said, "You looking for herb?"

"Yes," Kenji said. "Yes, we are."

I knew we were done for that minute.

The guy took our money and headed north. "He's not coming back," I said.

"I was just thinking that," Kenji said. "What's so funny?"

I was laughing. I felt oddly very good. I had the rare feeling of earning some firsthand wisdom. I could hear myself telling the story to friends at a party, like Carly relating something that she'd never ever let happen again. Kenji and I stood there making fun of ourselves as the northern Manhattan sky got chalky and pink. *Thanks for your help, sir. How very sweet of you to ask. That's exactly what we want — herb. Herb, indeed!*

"Hello. It's Ellie." I say to Kenji's mom. "Happy Thanksgiving."

"We've got a number of people over," she says. She doesn't like me very much anymore. She thinks we're up to no good. She caught us lying together on Kenji's bed—fully clothed. Every song on the radio that day talked about spooning, and we were curious what the big deal was about. I can't imagine how anyone could actually fall asleep that way; my breath sounded so loud, it alone could have kept me awake. "Isn't your family spending the day together?"

"We are. We're with my sister's boyfriend's family on the Island. Actually, it's her fiancé." I dig the heel of my shoe into the driveway gravel until small bits of rock and dirt slip in. "We're spending the day with her fiancé."

I'm not exactly sure why I say this, I just know it's something Kenji's mom will get off on. "Oh! I didn't realize your sister was getting married."

"I guess she is." I wonder if it's possible that she's married already. I wonder if she'd do that without telling me.

"How wonderful! Congratulate your family for me!"

"Okay," I say, and she goes off to get Kenji. I can hear her calling him.

"What's up?" he asks. "How was the bird?"

"I haven't even seen it yet. I don't think we'll ever get home."

"Call me when you walk the dog and I'll come down. We can smoke a smoke."

"All right."

"My uncle is here from Atlanta," Kenji says. "We've spent the last two hours talking about how Coca-Cola has the technology to project its logo on the moon. The only holdup is that it'll interfere with air traffic. He's so fucked up, but he gave me a tin of Nat Sherman's while my mother wasn't looking, so we'll smoke up. Okay?"

"Okay." I slip my shoes off and spill out the rocks.

"I gotta go," he says.

"Kenji?"

"Yeah?"

I don't know exactly what I want to say. I don't feel anything romantic like Carly wants to believe. I just feel like it's urgent that he be my friend forever. Sometimes I look at him and think: We're in this together. Remember, we're in this together. It's the way Carly is supposed to look at me. "I'll just see you later," I say.

I hang up and lie on the gravel for a while longer. It's aching to get dark. Every bush and tree looks like it's slipping on another layer, something a little warmer and gray. I am hoping that Carly will come looking for me, that she alone will find me on the far side of the car. She'll say, *What are you doing, you freak!*

And as my teeth chatter and my neck catches all kinds of draft, I'll point to the big white cheek of the moon and say, *Look.*

Amazing, she'll say. She'll lie down next to me. We'll spread out our mother's coat, her arm in one sleeve, mine in the other, and with our bare arms in the center we'll pass a cigarette back and forth and watch the moon glow enormous in the still-light sky, rising as it darkens, shifting from something mammoth and spectacular to just regular old moon by the time anyone else comes by. But I only wait about two more minutes. It's cold and I know she's not coming.

Back inside, Mom, Dad, and Carly are all sitting together on one couch in the darkening living room. The only light is coming from the glass doors behind them. Sitting so close they look like the silhouette of a mountain range. They're in the middle of some conversation. A Miles Davis disc is still playing, the nursery school taunt of "So What?" I don't know where Mr. and Mrs. Shelby are, and I'm surprised Alex isn't hanging off my sister like a sidecar.

"Where have you been?" my mother asks.

"Nowhere."

"I can feel the cold coming off you," my father says. He holds out an afghan like it's a towel and I'm a toddler emerging naked from a bath.

"It's okay." I walk past all of them to the glass doors to look at the backyard again, its thickening tree line about an acre away. The wind picks up and the naked trees are swaying slowly around the edge of the grass, like dancers skirting a stage. Last year when we did Thanksgiving in San Francisco, Carly snuck me out of the hotel and into a peep show in North Beach. She was writing a paper on gender roles and subverting traditional power dynamics. I couldn't believe she got me in.

We stood close together, giggling, in a dark tiny booth. Don't touch anything, she told me. I kept my hands balled up in my sleeves. As long as Carly kept putting in quarters, the electronic shade stayed up to display a bunch of swaying girls, naked, bored, waiting for something to happen. That's what I'm thinking about as I look out on the Shelbys' backyard, how last Thanksgiving Carly and I were running around North Beach and, at one in the morning, drinking flavored sodas at an Italian café.

"So we're talking about visiting your sister in the spring," my mother says. "How would you like a spring weekend in Maine?"

I don't even turn around. The sky is bleeding the color out of itself; even the silhouettes are starting to disappear.

"It sounds like a terrific time, Ellie," my father says. "Carly was telling us about the new Roller Derby in Portland. She'll probably try to get us all out on the floor."

Carly laughs, the laugh that makes dad feel like he's still a young and dangerous guy. Then she says to me: "What's with you, Miss Grumpy-Poo?"

"Nothing," I say and sit down close to my mom. I know Carly will think I'm sulking like a baby, and I know I'll be embarrassed about it later, but she can't see my face and I can't see hers. It's dark enough that I can hardly see the furniture. This used to happen all the time, summers at the beach. We've spent a million nights talking after dinner as a room went dark and no one would think to turn on the lights. The change was slow and our eyes could adjust; we never lost sight of each other. Out the window now, I can make out Venus and the still-huge moon but I don't point it out. I just watch it and half-listen to the plans they're all making.

"Why are you all sitting here in the dark?" Alex steps into the room and snaps on the light. It's a shock he wields, a disruption. My whole family is sitting close together on one couch looking at him, a nest of newborn chicks blinking. Carly smiles, not at Alex or at us but to herself. It's like she's a million miles away. I have no idea at all what she's thinking.

We all follow Mrs. Shelby into the dining room. She has lit candles and the light off the table cloth is kicking up an orange glow. Or maybe that's coming off the bird, a beautiful golden brown, or the tangerine salad, bruising with beets.

"Oh." My mother rests her hand at the base of her throat. "It couldn't be more beautiful."

Everyone nods, reaching to pull out chairs and take their seats, but all I can think is, *Yes it could.* It could absolutely be more beautiful. I think about the four of us trudging up and down the ridiculous hills last year in San Francisco. Carly and I ran ahead of our parents to the top of Twin Peaks. The city spread out on all sides below us, and Carly directed my attention beyond the Victorians to the bridges and beaches, to her favorite café and where she rode her bike in the afternoons. There was so much wind, I could hardly see. Carly held my hair back to keep it out of my eyes. She stood behind me like that, holding my ponytail like it was a rudder, and we laughed as she turned us in circles, like we were one person, to see the whole view. As we looked, she rested her cheek on the top of my head, and even through the breeze, I could feel the warmth of her undivided affections.

Bike
New York!

The ride was forty-two miles, covered five boroughs, and twenty-eight thousand people were expected to participate. The Bike New York! brochure said nothing about beer,
but because he was getting married at the end of the month,
lately everything Derek did with his buddies involved beer. Beer
and lap dancing. Beer and breasts.

The party plans for this ride purported merely to include pit
stops at bars in every borough to celebrate the pending wedding—or was it to celebrate the last golden days of bachelorhood?
Derek wasn't quite sure. At each prior bachelor event there had
been a toast—a cheerful and heartfelt meeting of glasses—and
then, emerging from behind the bar, under the table, beneath the

sails on Gary's boat for god's sake, there were suddenly women peeling off panties, shimmying out of skirts, so many women moving toward him.

And while Derek recalled feeling awkward and undone, shy at each celebration, his face in all the photos registered in a grimace, a smirk—the face of a guy accustomed to the world performing for his benefit, the face of an asshole he'd never imagined himself to be. So despite his soft spot for the adolescent biathlon of sporting and drinking, he couldn't seem to get himself out of bed for the ride.

The rain, he reasoned, could serve as his excuse. Even from his bed he could see large drops plucking off the fire escape railing outside his window. The phone rang at 7:30, 8:00, and again at 8:15. He listened as the messages came in over the machine. "Hey, buddy!" and "Get up, guy!" and, eventually, "Listen, man. At 8:30 we're gone."

The sky was still gray and damp when, finally, at twenty past eight, he got out of bed and stood in the window of his second-floor walk-up. Across the street, at the mouth of the Eighty-Sixth Street subway, he watched a clump of people and bicycles untangle themselves, making a calm, if slow, procession down the stairs. Derek imagined the awkward hoisting of bikes over turnstiles, the tired quiet of the riders, the good-natured quips about the rain. He had always liked the hushed camaraderie of a daunting expedition.

He watched a young woman in a yellow slicker stop just before the subway entrance. She rested her bike against her body and arched back to look deep and far into the sky. She turned in a circle, wheeling the bike around her as she spun, reminding Derek of street contortionists he had seen once in France, performing with cups out to collect thin, clinking change. In the last few years, he'd traveled a lot, alone. At just thirty he was the last of his friends to get married, the holdout, the wild man. A ridiculous idea—his own parents had been past his age when they'd first met—but he played along. He'd always been mischievous and athletic, the first kid to scale the steeple, to dive from a tree-top into a shallow bay. And now, as a last vestige of this, with a little encouragement and booze, he could still pull off the occasional act of sinew and charm.

Derek saw the woman outside smile as if discerning a hint of sun somewhere high, high above. Her neck was long and thrown back, stretching, and something tugged at him. He'd been looking forward to this ride. The friends who'd known him longest and best would be waiting for him, ready to bolster in Derek everything that performed well in sport. If he hurried, he reasoned, either he'd find his friends, or just go it alone—meet his group at the message board at the Staten Island finish line. What was a little rain after all?

He opted out of the subway, choosing instead to course straight down Second Avenue, bouncing over potholes, cutting around pokey buses. He slowed as he passed his fiancée's third-floor window—her blinds were open; she liked to wake to sunlight. He could go there later. He could sleep there tonight. His heart began to thump. Why hadn't he just gotten up in time?

When he arrived at the meeting place under the scaffolding by Battery Park, there was no one from his group, just a girl in a raincoat—hood up and checking her watch. She was leaning against an Italian road bike with souped-up components—high-pressure tires, a carbon-fiber fork, and Z-back comfort arm brackets that shot up like a skyscraper from the horizon of her handlebars.

Derek was riding a twenty-one-speed mountain bike that had seen trails in the White Mountains, the Smokies, the long, wide highways of Montana. Both he and the girl wore yellow pullover rain jackets. They stood out from the dreary morning like unbroken egg yolks on a breakfast plate.

"Hi," said Derek. "Did you see a bunch of guys here? Four of them? I'm late."

"No. My people must have left too." She looked up. Her hair was tucked back into her hood, but Derek could see that it was thick and dark, dyed somewhere between burgundy and red. She squinted from the rain as she searched the clouds, which were low and sinking down onto the city. She beamed as though she had, in fact, seen a promise of sunshine—of something—to come. Was she the same girl?

Derek looked around, past the trees of Battery Park dripping with rain and new spring green, past the oxidized copper lampposts, past the telescopes along the water that—for just a quarter—could bring the Statue of Liberty into view. The girl brought a hand to her face, nibbled a cuticle and looked up at him expectantly, "What do you think? Do you want to go anyway?"

Were his friends behind this—behind the dumpster up the path, huddled in back of the newsstand, under an awning across the street? He could imagine them lunging out at any moment, making lewd gestures, whisking Derek and this young girl away— bikes and helmets and all—to Bob's office just up Broadway, or to Mike's place on Church Street, or to some overpriced steakhouse near the Federal Building with a private room in back.

"Fuck!" Derek huffed to himself, but there the word was, outside of his mouth and saturating the air along with the rain.

"Fuck what?" the girl turned her face up to his. At six foot two, he had about eight inches on her. Her eyes were big and brown and wide open.

"I just should have been here earlier." He wiped rain from his face with his sleeve and the fabric caught on the reddish growth of his stubble. "I was supposed to meet friends."

"Me too. I was supposed to meet people from school."

"Which school?" Derek assumed a college—NYU, Pratt, Hunter.

"Hudson High School," she said, laughing, unzipping her jacket to reveal the school name and the eagle printed on her sweatshirt. "I'm a junior. Almost done."

"Oh." Derek moved the word around his mouth in a drawn-out loop of sarcasm. Like a high school kid himself, he still used sarcasm when feeling insecure. How could he have guessed she was in high school?

"You know, I think I saw you this morning. Did you take the train here from Eighty-Sixth?" He asked hopefully, as though such a coincidence would excuse his dishonorable imagination.

"No," she said. "It couldn't have been me. I'm coming from somewhere else. I'm Serena."

"I'm Derek." He looked all around. If his friends were watching right now, they'd be laughing at him.

"I think we should just go," she said, and Derek looked at her, trying to determine if there was a come-on—a promise and threat contained in her words—but Serena just checked her tires, giving each a quick squeeze, a pinch between her thumb and forefinger.

"We can keep an eye out for our people," she continued, "but if we stick together we can have a buddy system—you know, watch each other's bikes when we have to stop and use the john."

It was so reasonable, Derek thought—exactly the kind of plan his fiancée Jill would endorse. Imagine if he were out somewhere in Queens and stepped out of a portable toilet to find his bike stolen. Or worse, what if—to avoid just such a heist—he got a ticket for taking a leak out on some street? "What were you thinking?" Jill would laugh. "Why didn't you team up with somebody, have some company? Or at least bring a lock?"

"Let's go," Derek said, pushing off the curb without a look back.

They went. They nosed through the scatter of late-departing cyclists. Derek scanned the crowd for his friends, even though he knew they'd be far past this last departing heat, largely composed of families with kids and training wheels and bicycles built for two. Here, the ride was rife with unfamiliar challenges: There were special bikes for the handicapped propelled by arm power; a pedicab towed a woman on crutches; a father pulled his family over and took requests in front of the Donut Hole.

"Look at that." Serena pointed up the canyons of Sixth Avenue ahead, where the street clumped with the sloped backs of cyclists heading into Central Park. Even steering with one hand, Serena rode steadily, pointedly, with the same ease as Jill coming in the front door after work, depositing the key on the hook, mail on the table, Tupperware in the sink, a hand on Derek's arm, his thigh— an unwavering flow of purpose and motion. "We're behind all the fun."

Derek nodded. He knew that up ahead—in the thick of it— the crowd would be pulsing with hoots and enthusiasm, team T-shirts, boom boxes, even a beer helmet or two.

She talked.

In the park she told him she was a Sagittarius and that she was saving up to get her chart done. She told him her friends would be irritated with her, that if she carried a cell phone like everybody else she would have been able to meet up with her group. "It's ridiculous though," she said, shaking her head and riding beside him. "No one should be able to reach you 24-7."

Derek laughed. It amazed him how difficult it was in New York to disappear completely. Once he'd escaped to Glacier National Park for a week, biked the Rockies, outsmarted the bears, and tented up with a hiker named Lily for the weekend. He almost began a recount but stopped himself; he hated to sound like a has-been, in love with his own reckless once-upon-a-times. Instead he said nothing, just listened to his tires picking up moisture, kicking mud and water up against his jacketed back. Vines hung down from overpasses, directing drops at his nose with the precision of a wand. They passed the carousel, the obelisk, the Harlem Meer riding silently, legs pumping in quick, sure revolutions.

In the Bronx, across the Madison Avenue Bridge, they stopped at a rest area to eat quartered oranges and bananas just as the Bike New York! staff was cleaning up rinds and peels, breaking down the repair stand, and shouting out a call to get moving. Derek waited for Serena in front of the portable toilets, both his bike and hers leaned against his hip. He eyed the broken blacktop of the streets, the gates pulled down over the row of storefronts, not a single thing open on a Sunday. He could see the back of the billboards he'd long admired from the roadway, the steel lettering in reverse, the words backwards. He hadn't been anywhere new in a while.

Now, in Brooklyn, twenty-eight miles into the ride, with the great long stretch of the Belt Parkway before them, they rode past the two-family houses at roof level as though on some Disney-land monorail track. The gray road stretched ahead in a slight and steady grade upward.

"So," said Serena, growing restless and impatient—they had been riding in silence for hours now—"next weekend there's a ride from Manhattan to Montauk. A hundred miles. How much GustoGranola is that?"

"Next weekend I'm getting married," Derek said. "At the Puck Building at seven on Saturday." He added the last information as though it were an invitation, as though Serena should consider, if she had nothing better to do, stopping by for a little champagne and dinner.

"Then why aren't you riding with your girl?"

"Jill wanted to do it. She would have done it. Maybe we'll do it together next year, but this ride was supposed to be just one in a series of bachelor party events. Except that I woke up today and couldn't handle any more bachelor party anything."

"So you're getting married," Serena said emphatically. She bit her lip, looking curious. Or was it mournful? Derek considered the possibility. It could be a look of jealousy, of longing. He'd recently run in to an old girlfriend and mentioned his engagement, and she'd had that look, hadn't she?

"Do you have a cake yet?" Serena asked.

"I don't know. I haven't been that involved in the planning."

He had, in fact, spent hours tasting cakes and hearing bands. He'd even helped pick out the place settings. He'd been *very* involved in the planning, but more than anything else, he'd focused on Jill—the way she kept the details all straight, the way she raised her eyebrows at a rip-off, how she threatened to take her business elsewhere. He'd known a lot of women in his life, but he'd never noticed any who had been so able. It most often rendered him silent, fascinating him, somehow filling him up, but that felt small now, here in the damp gray of Brooklyn, with his heart pumping in sport and his oldest friends whooping it up just around the next turn, or the next.

"Well, you must have a cake if the wedding's next week, but I wish you didn't. My parents have a bakery and my mom makes the most amazing cakes. She really does. She's been in magazines."

"Oh yeah?"

"They're not far from here," Serena was eager, pedaling fast and close beside him. "We could go look. It'd be quick. We could take a shortcut later and catch back up with the ride."

"You want to go to your parents' place?"

She nodded. She had a beautiful smile.

"Are you sure you should be inviting strange men off the beaten path? Don't they teach you that in school?"

"I trust you." She looked right at him, smiling, her eyebrows raised in a threat or a dare. It was still possible, he thought, to discover a truly great cake, to pay extra and have it made in time.

"Come on," she said, reminding him of so many girls he'd

known—the jaded girls, the willing, the brave, and the naïve—a compendium of familiar gestures and body parts. Except, he reminded himself, she was only a child.

He wasn't sure what to do. "Okay," he said. "Let's go have a look."

Derek followed Serena down the service road that ran abreast of the B.Q.E. The roadside scrub grass was littered with glass shards and faded soda cans, but its new spring green shoots nearly glowed amidst the trash, showing a color too tender for exposure, like new skin under a scab. He'd grown up around Manhattan money and always felt a guilty determination to know the whole city, to bike New York in its entirety. He'd always hated thinking of himself as confined. He yanked up on his handlebars to jump over a pothole, a move he'd been practicing since he was a kid. His muscles were tight; he was already sore.

They turned onto a small street and he followed Serena's hop onto the sidewalk. Two girls hula-hooped before a bakery storefront, wearing blue and orange Knicks shirts hanging to their knees. Serena got off her bicycle and leaned it against the building.

"Can you two watch these bikes for me?" She rolled her eyes at Derek. "These are my cousins. Welcome to munchkinland, right?"

"Hey," Derek said. He offered his hand and then thought better of it. How did you greet a girl so young? He had no idea.

Serena tugged at the neck of her sweatshirt and extracted a key on a string. She unlocked the front door and Derek took his first step into the bakery, toward the rich, sleepy smell of bread, of chocolate, of yeast.

A Formica counter connected to make an L shape with a long line of bakery cases. Beyond the glass panels were gold-tinted trays arranged neatly with doilies and tiny desserts—tarts topped with a single strawberry, a mound of raspberries, a kiwi slice. There were tiny napoleons, palm-sized cheesecakes, miniature éclairs, cream puffs drizzled with nuts and drops of green frosting. There were versions of the very same desserts in their standard sizes and then, toward the back of the store, a tall case hosted a wedding cake five tiers high and decorated down one side with a cascade of pastry-tubed bouquets, flouncy and complex as prom dresses. There was no one behind the counter, just a table stacked with unfolded pastry boxes and a spool of red and white string hanging from the ceiling, which snapped intermittently in the current from the fan. "We don't open till four on Sunday," Serena explained.

Derek ran his fingers up and down the seams of his nylon shorts in a nervous and futile search for pockets. Serena hopped up onto the countertop near the register, spun neatly on her ass, and jumped off the other side. She was nimble, he thought, she was quick.

She pushed past a swinging door into the kitchen. "Mo-om," Serena called out. "Mom!"

Derek sat on the edge of a red padded chair with his legs parted, elbows on his knees, staring down at the gray flecks on the lino-leum tile. His calves ached and this suddenly felt like a miserable idea. The last thing he felt like doing was chatting up some girl's mom and getting bamboozled into buying something just to save face.

"Serena?" he called out, but there was no answer, just the whir of the mechanism behind the wall clock. Watch, he'd get stuck here all day, sampling butter-cream frosting and recounting his tales of wedding planning in New York like some giddy bride. *I'm ruined,* he'd say to Jill. *You've ruined me.* It was true, he realized suddenly. He missed his friends.

But then it occurred to him: What if there was no mom in the back, no dad? What if the back room was filled with his people, a big bunch of guys with another elaborate party plan? Everyone would be stepping out of the kitchen at any moment, Serena her-self emerging from a giant cake. There'd be high fives all around. Serena would sit on Derek's lap, eat frosting off his lip, draw her quick, lithe tongue along the edge of his ear. Gotcha, Steve-O would say. He'd give a big belly laugh, crack open a beer.

He'd known all along, really—his friends wouldn't have left him alone for this ride. He could be so insecure. It was shocking that still, even now, as an adult, as a man on the brink of mar-riage, he could feel as abandoned as a teen.

There was noise in the kitchen. Derek could hear it even above the fans—the clanging of pans, the squeaks of a wheeled cart in need of oil.

"I'm coming." Serena drew the words out and they grew louder, like a drumroll. He studied the world map taped to the wall and thought of all the places he'd still like to see: the Amazon, the Himalayas, the Everglades. God, there were so many places he still wanted to go.

"They're not here." Serena pushed open the swinging kitchen door with a kick at the base and a slam of her back against it. Her arms were full of binders, photo albums stacked just to her chest, Derek noticed, shelving her breasts. She laid the books on the counter before him. "My parents must have already left for my uncle's in Staten Island. They're barbecuing there so they can pick up me and my bike, so I don't have to ride all the way home."

"That's nice," Derek said. He was a little embarrassed and a little angry. "That's a nice parent thing to do."

"Baby will be tired." Serena pouted and pinched her own cheek. "Bring these to a table and I'll get us some snacks. What do you want? The mini cheesecakes are the best, but I'm afraid they'll make us cramp when we get back to biking. Maybe we'll split one of those and just stick with sugar: go all chocolate and tarts."

She pulled a large tray out from under the counter and began walking the stretch of cases, expertly sliding open the doors, reaching into the displays and extracting pastries without fumbling or looking, without hesitation. She ducked under the hinged section of the counter and delivered the assortment to the booth Derek had selected.

"Wow," he said, shy and delighted. He wasn't used to not knowing how to act around women—or girls—and maybe, he considered, in this distinction lay the problem. "What a spread."

Serena plucked a glazed kiwi slice off a tiny tart, popped it in her mouth, and poised her fingers above a halved strawberry. "Yum," she said.

Derek contemplated the heaping plate and selected a mini mud cake. Serena slid deeper into the booth, turned to lean against the wall, and stretched her legs down the bench seat. She broke a little Napoleon in half and inspected the layers of filling before taking a bite, as though she might have thrown the whole thing away had she not been happy with what she saw inside.

"You must win a lot of friends with this place." Derek imagined the booths filling with her friends late at night, a picket fence of skateboards propped up by the door, the dessert trays raided by stoned kids with the munchies. He imagined weekends with her parents out of town, how the jukebox must play all night, how couples must make out leaning against the cool cases.

"Puh-lease," Serena said, tossing half her pastry back onto the plate. "Only the teachers care. They just want me to bring stuff for the holiday parties."

"Bullshit," he said, wanting to prove he knew the score.

"Maybe." She shrugged. "But let's get to the business."

She pushed the plate out of the way and slid the stack of photo albums in front of Derek. "Since the family's all out at my uncle's, I can just show you the wedding catalogs, and you can see if there's anything that might interest you, and you could either order now or go home and discuss it with your, with your Jill, and come back or call or, uh, whatever." Serena giggled.

"What do you do, anyway?" she asked casually, flipping open an album, turning it sideways so she and Derek could lean in to share a view.

"Law," he said, knowing it was enough of an answer; it was just a money question but he went on anyway. "A lot of copyright stuff, patents. I always thought I'd do advocacy though, lobbying. But you never know how it'll go."

"Oh," she said, frankly, bored. It was a little boring. But that was the funny thing about finding your way in the world. There was a place laid out for you, he thought, and even as you stepped into it, happy for the chance to rest, you wondered how you ever ended up there.

Serena began a slow turning of pages. Under the cellophane of each sheet was an eight-by-ten black-and-white photo of a cake—some on display at actual weddings, some just shot atop the bakery counter. Derek dully watched the pictures pass. How did you end up anywhere and why, he thought. Why had he ended up here?

"This is my favorite." Serena said. She slapped her hand against the page to get his attention.

Derek looked at the picture. It was of a big cake on a wooden picnic table. The cake was four tiers high and set on a bed of ivy, all of it dappled with sunlight through the trees above. The spots of brightness and shadow made the cake look somehow sadly illuminated, like stained glass, shining from within.

"That was my sister's wedding," Serena offered. "It was upstate. It was summer. It was nice."

"Your sister's wedding?" Derek repeated uncertainly, as if this were his first date, as if he'd never had a conversation with a girl before. "Did everyone go? Did your family close the store?"

"For the weekend. We all went, but I took the pictures. It was all on me."

"You took this?"

"Yeah. I take all the cakes." She winked at him. "I get forty a photo, and I print them in the darkroom at school. The wedding, I let them give me money for supplies, but I just did it free. You know, family."

"Sure." Derek flipped through the album.

"That's what I want to study. That's what I want to do at college—not cake pictures but real stuff. You want to see my real stuff?"

Before he could answer she'd extracted a slick gray pocket folder from the back of the book and slid it before him. "Look."

Derek opened the folder and looked through the heavy, curling prints. He too had done high school photography, striding through the hallways, confident with props—long lenses, flashbulbs, cigarettes. Girls would pose, huddling close, curls colliding. He remembered their bracelets, how at picnics, at the beach, smoking on the steps, the silver bands would catch sunlight and shine.

There were night shots up Broadway, just a streak of headlights across the dark. There were shots of storefronts and fire hydrants taken around the neighborhood. And there was a Chinatown series—featuring ducks dangling in restaurant windows, pagoda phone booths, a dense crowd bursting forth from small subway stairs. There was, of course, the requisite photo of fish on ice.

He wasn't sure what kind of fish they were, but each was about a foot long, and they were all stacked high in a pyramid atop a bed of ice. The eyes were perfect circles—wide and just short of lifeless. On the right side of the frame, one fish hung just below the rest of his row, looking like it was about to slide from the pile and escape off the bottom of the page. *Whoops!* Derek felt like exclaiming.

"I like this," he said.

"You do?"

He nodded.

"Everyone likes that one. Why does everyone like that one? I can't figure out what I actually did right."

"Well," said Derek. The picture was printed poorly, underexposed. The focus was clear though: the drying scales, the light catching the ice, the eye that seemed—even as you looked—to slip further down the pile, heading for the floor and a dangerous getaway. *Whoops!*

He hoped to say something thoughtful and profound, maybe something about the virtues of distinguishing oneself from the heap, or about how the world loves a good renegade, but when he noticed Serena's eager face and how she looked so undeniably young, so curious, and, frankly, so *entitled* to counsel, he didn't feel like saying anything at all. "I don't know." He shrugged, like he, too, was nothing more than a child.

He could be anywhere in all the boroughs right now, he thought. He could be biking hard and fast, a little buzzed, among friends and after some personal best. "I want to get going," he said. He lowered his eyes down to her breasts and, in the silence, he let them linger there.

Serena laughed when she noticed, a flush spreading up along her cheeks and under the fine hairs that had slipped from her ponytail. She grabbed the photos and slid them out of sight onto the seat beside her. "I didn't mean to be boring." She wouldn't look up.

She yanked a napkin from the dispenser to give a quick wipe across the table. Then she took their plate to the sink behind the counter, leaving him alone with cake crumbs in his lap and the whirring of the clock. All she wanted was a little encouragement, a quick flurry of attention and awe. Why hadn't he just said something? Was that really too much for him to give?

"Hey, Serena," he called out, but she ignored him. She turned the water on, pumped at the soap dispenser, and he watched her back as she washed their single plate.

He looked at his face in the reflection of the chrome napkin dispenser. Distorted, his forehead was high, as though his hair had already receded, and his eyes appeared dark, drooping, and old. He thought of Jill, and of his parents, and of his in-laws arriving on Tuesday, flying clear across the country to give away their girl. He was a grown man, for god's sake; could he really still be such an asshole?

"Come on," Serena said. "Let's get out of here."

Outside, he watched Serena lock up the door, give a cookie to each of the cousins, and then mount her bike. He watched her now, pedaling ahead, leaving him just the view of her backside and her trailing shoelace, which dragged along the ground and snapped behind her foot as she rode, threatening to catch and tangle in her gears. She was just a kid—a very pretty, athletic, bubbly kid. How could he begrudge her that little show-and-tell? He felt compelled to confess to Serena every dirty thought he'd had. He felt compelled to arm her with everything he knew.

"Hey wait," he called out. "Stop."

When she did, he got off his own bike and knelt beside hers; he'd never felt quite so inept before. He picked up her right foot and rested it on his bent leg. "Here I am," he said, unsure, "in Brooklyn, on bended knee, and I am tying your shoe." An odd calm settled in his chest as he did it, and he could feel his own father's presence, as if he'd just stepped into the man's skin.

"C'mon," Serena said lightly. She gave her leg a small, coy kick and smiled down at him.

"Thank you for the cake," he said emphatically. "Thank you for the show."

Jill, he'd say, as soon as he got home, *what an amazing day.*

They caught up with the ride on the long stretch of the dull gray Gowanus. The road offered nothing in the way of views. To the right there was just steely water and wire fencing clogged inches high with trash blown from the highway. To the left was the same clot of deciduous trees and scrub grass that reminded Derek of his road trip back from Montana and the way the land lost splendor and offered nothing but the simple familiarity of a return home.

He slowed, his thighs growing stiff and bulky. The Verrazano Narrows Bridge went on forever, never seeming to crest. Three times Serena shot past him and then waited ahead until finally she zipped off to a peak on the horizon he couldn't seem to see.

Inevitably, he knew, he would remember this day no matter what had happened. It was, after all, the last weekend before his wedding, a wedding for which, even as he rode, he was becoming more and more excited.

He wished for a moment that he had stolen that fish photo, asked for a copy. Why hadn't he? He could have slipped it into the back of his shorts so it would lie under his jacket flat against him as he rode. He could have cut out that single slipping fish and kept it in his breast pocket at the wedding ceremony, placed the wide-eyed head poking out instead of a pocket square. *Whoops!* He could say it with a lilt as he lifted Jill's veil. She might think he was joking, feeling clumsy with the delicate tulle, but only he would know he was recalling something he'd felt today: a shift in lighting, a realignment of composition as he slipped from the point of focus in his own life.

As he rode on he contemplated the lever of his legs—how each move they made cranked the pedals, advanced the chain, turned the wheels, and propelled him forward, displacing air and creating wind. Far ahead, light seemed finally to be breaking through the clayey clouds, and Derek was pretty sure he could see Serena marking a crest to the bridge. She had her yellow jacket back on and it billowed around her as she pedaled into the wind. She seemed nearly to be floating on the pillow of her radiant jacket. Light shone through the fabric harnessing the glow around her like a lantern's shade. "That was you once," he encouraged himself, pedaling steadily. "See that, friend? That was once you."

The
Marrying
Kind

I'm wearing beige. It has taken months to come
to this conclusion: to go neutral, to come to no conclusion at all. I
feared black was bitter, and green was envious, and yellow might
connote my own reluctance to get hitched. Red, of course, was
out of the question, and I figured I'd let Laura have white to herself. The beige I'm wearing is a muddy beige, maybe even more
of a brown. I have never, ever been a bad sport.

It is a happy day. Jay and his bride are far across the room,
his hand on the small of her back, his cheek in the clutches of
Laura's mother. I've never seen Jay in a tuxedo before, and the
long, graceful line of him looks handsome, in spite of, if not because of, his right pant leg being tucked somehow into his sock,

as if he might have to hop on a bike at any moment and pedal quickly away.

During his grand tour of the room, Jay has twice taken his attention from Laura and her kin to look around and find me— once when I was by the dance floor discussing perennials with his mother, once at the bar while getting a shot glass of olives, and now, again, leaning against the wall beside his best friend, Drew. Jay smiles and his wrist flexes, a flinch of a wave in my direction.

I toast him, my pig-in-a-blanket raised high in the air. We have not actually spoken yet today.

He called just last week to tell me about Laura having a trellis built so all the couples could stand by it and have Polaroids taken. I nearly said, "Swell!" and nearly told him I was pregnant, nearly said I'd be bringing a date after all.

"You're not just marrying the prettiest schoolteacher in town," I reminded him instead, "She was also high school prom chair, wasn't she?"

"You're going to laugh. Just promise you won't let her hear you laugh."

"I won't," I said, "I really won't," and when he and Laura stood kissing on the pulpit, nothing was funny at all. Drew took my hand and we slipped out the side door, skipping the hugs and receiving line.

I've had five years to imagine this wedding, Jay managing to extend the engagement every spring, like he's perpetually renewing a library book. I pictured the balloons right, and the meringues, and the sidelong glances across the room until later in the day when we might sneak in a quick kiss by the coatrack. I pictured the quaint church service and this six-piece band, but never did I imagine I'd be standing here pregnant, my body forming placenta while I'm making small talk by the buffet.

I talked to the kid the whole drive from New York this morning, pointing out sights over corn nuts and juice. I said, "This is beautiful downtown Hartford, Evie, insurance capital of the world.

"Here we are, Isabelle, the Greater Boston area. Just to the east is where Jay and I went to college and just to the west is where you were conceived.

"Bienvenue au New Hampshire, Veronica. That means 'Welcome' in French. We're welcome! Say thank you. Now let's get there in time to see your father get hitched."

I wasn't supposed to get pregnant. I mean, no one gets pregnant on her "funnymoon," a last hurrah with her old boyfriend before he ties the knot. But then I guess most people don't get a funnymoon where it really is funny and they really do moon, swimming naked through phosphorescents at night.

From the very beginning I said, "I'm not keeping you, kid." I called up the doctor with the home test still in hand, desperate and blue as the oxygen-deprived.

"Look," she said. "You're hardly too young to seriously consider whether or not you want kids."

"Right now?" I asked, my heart thrumming double-time, beating, it seemed, suddenly for two. "Or do you mean ever?"

"Give yourself a couple of weeks. We can't even find the embryo much less remove it before then."

This is modern science! It's unbelievable. They've found the mysterious ancient squid that for centuries has lived undetected off the coast of Australia. They can pinpoint predisposition to obesity and Huntington's chorea when they're just penciled-in appointments on the date books of our genes. They can find all that but not my fertilized egg in a uterus that can't be more than three inches wide.

"Just relax," the doctor counseled. "Be yourself. Think things through. Be with friends."

So here I am. For a moment this morning, the whole ordeal seemed too much to handle and I nearly threw the beige shoes back into the closet and said, "Kid, we're staying home." But it was already a clear, bright day—perfect for a drive. The car started right up, there was no traffic on the bridge, and I figured that after all my bravado, *not* showing up might be the strangest move of all. Besides, this was it—the last chance to parade the possibilities, to shout out objections over "Here Comes the Bride."

Now Drew and I are standing in the corner by the puff pastries, two swinging singles making jelly-bean jokes. There are handfuls strewn across each tabletop, bubblegum flavor, we've deduced. They are on the cocktail napkins, the matchbooks, and the hand towels in the bathroom—small pink splotches, kidney-shaped and pert. Whenever Jay and I talked about getting married, the plans were for eloping to Vegas at the Elvis House of Love or throwing a barbecue in a vacant lot and getting a Ramones cover band to play. We were young then, sure, but this comes too far.

Laura has opened Jay's jacket, revealing to her friends his pink cummerbund. She explains and points like it is a courtroom exhibit, the very evidence of his love apparent in the simple fact that he's wearing pink. I can't decide if it's repulsive of Jay or absolutely gorgeous that he's in love enough to be playing this role, her rumpled but willing dress-me-up doll. "Love like that is hard to find," I tell Drew, faking wonder and envy at once.

Drew, the unapologetic perpetual bachelor, thirty-six and still schtupping college kids, is checking out the band of she-cousins roosting at a table. "Love is never hard to find," he says. "What's really hard to find is both socks in the morning." He gives me a wink as he heads for a pink taffeta rump, passing me the rest of his stuffed mushroom cap.

For a long time it didn't even occur to me that this Laura thing would last. First Jay called her simple-but-convenient, then limited-but-earnest, and obvious-but-enthusiastic. Finally, I guess, all the buts won out.

By the time I met Laura, she and Jay had already been dating two years. I was in a group show of documentary photography at a little gallery in Cambridge and Jay brought Laura to the opening, which, at the time, I fancied as all part of the fun: Jay and I would pretend there was nothing between us, and I'd get to check out the other woman occupying his time. How comic it would be to recount later on!

But there was a moment, I admit it, when I lost my breath in panic. Jay was halfway through the front door, Laura still behind him, unseen and mysterious for just a few seconds more. I felt a fear so sudden and pure it was physically painful, anxiety like a harness wrenching my shoulder blades. But she was Laura. She trailed behind Jay like a little girl, alternately looking to him for approval and then sending him off to fetch her more wine and cheese.

My pictures were of the Army Corps of Engineers battling beach erosion, building up jetties along the East Coast. I'd caught sight of the oddly solemn procession of enormous, solitary boulders being driven along the beach, each strapped onto a separate flatbed truck. "I don't get why they bother," said Laura. "Eventually it erodes."

Jay explained how the jetties work like arms trapping sand in a hug, letting it collect instead of washing away.

"But eventually." She kept at it in a singsong meant to be flirtatiously defiant. *But eventually.* She was giddy with her own insistence and, I imagine, all that free-flowing rosé.

"She's a little ridiculous," I told Jay.

"But she's loyal," he defended. "But she's mine."

Of course I wonder sometimes what his excuse has been for me.

Laura's friends are all sneaking peeks in my direction, their expressions a combination of sympathy and distrust. They are rightfully prickly with intuition, and they are having a tough time figuring out my role. Whether they've got me pegged as a contemptible harlot or simply Jay's college ex lost out on a good man, it makes little sense to them that I'd be here today. They approach all at once, a gaggle of accusatory bridesmaids, the most honored stepping out to the fore, "If you haven't lived in Boston for ten years," she asks without introduction, "how do you know Drew here so well?"

"Oh, I've visited," I say, but I don't tell how often or where it is that I've slept.

The last decade boils down to any number of things. A visit every season is a hundred nights in the same bed, two thousand hours together, three hundred coffees at Dunkin' Donuts, four weeks' time behind the wheel, all giddy in the gut and weak in the knees. We've spent enough sleepy-eyed daybreaks at the beach right across the street from this room for me to track the changing fit of sweaters I've bought him—hanging off his shoulder blades in active summers or pulling over his winter paunch.

We have gone on too long to make excuses, too long to imagine how the whole thing could ever end. I smile at Laura's friends, shake hands, and say, "Nice to meet you." Then I head for the reassuring line of strangers at the bar.

Not long ago I told Jay, "I can't feel bad about this anymore. You're the one getting married. Feeling bad is your job now."

He rolled over on his back and thought for a while. "She wants to get married and I do love her," he said. "What can I say? I just love you too." That's just how he said it, like a man who had made up his mind to not make up his mind. In this way, we have always been very much alike.

———————

So far the best part of this wedding is that no one has asked me if I'm doin' okay. It's all I've heard from my friends since the invitation arrived. There must have been all-night speed dialing across the continents, all horror and fear for uncoupled me. Are you doin' okay? I mean really, you doin' okay?

Yes, I'm doing okay. Of course I'm doing okay.

I'm attributing this new panic to my birthday on Monday. It's the end of the world it seems, now that I'm turning thirty-three. For the longest time I thought women at thirty-three went nuts, organically, age triggering some biological wellspring of panic. Now I understand it's all pressure from the increasing married majority who can be so damn uncomfortable with a woman alone.

I'm starting to worry that I'll get caught up in the hype, waking up one day in an always-dressed-right fury to hustle from work to drinks with Mr. Might-Be-Right. In my twenties I always had bosses who'd do that—it didn't matter if it was at *Mademoiselle* or *National Geographic*. They'd turn thirty-three and start bringing changes of outfits to work and then, hungover and unfulfilled, spend most days harassing the receptionist. On Friday, I told my studio intern to be warned, that I'd not only be returning pensive from the Last Wedding but I'd also be coming back thirty-three. Jake said he'd set me up with his stepbrother, who has a "super sweet spot for arty middle-aged women."

"Middle-aged?" I said. "Haven't you heard that life expectancy has increased, that we're all supposed to push a hundred and one?"

"Life is long," my mother and father say. "Be with someone. Don't you want to be part of something bigger than yourself?"

"Of course," I say.

It's just that I always think these moments should count: I'm in a huddle with all of Jay's friends who have grown up together in this same small town. We've all settled together into a huge "kids" table and I'm not the new kid anymore. More than a few of Jay's friends have called in the last few weeks to make sure I'd be coming, to offer places to stay, to say things like, would've-could've-should've been you.

Laura comes by, all long curls and lavender ribbons, and says, "Now kids, are we being good?"

We are being good, all of us. Laramie has not said in his radio-announcer voice, "Jay Hansen, MIT biologist, marries proud owner of New England's biggest TV"; Jeff has kept his cost analysis of the wedding to himself; and all of Drew's jokes have been about the bridesmaids. It is as if everyone, for this single day, is in tacit agreement not to make fun.

Laura says, "All right. Eat up now." Then she makes fast back to Jay's side, leaving all of us smiling despite ourselves. I'm even doing it. I'm sitting here stretching out these cheeks and thinking she's one terrific loyal gal. That she'll make one terrific loyal wife. One terrific loyal mom. I'm suddenly not feeling too well.

The best view of the ocean has ended up in the bathroom of the banquet hall. From the window I can see a wide scoop of the short New Hampshire coastline, and I can read the beach like a pack of tarot cards, spread out to organize what I already know.

At the north end of the cove I had my first "lobstah roll" and learned to describe it as "wicked good."

We'd drive here from Boston in college and do it just around the bend, on the beach, making jokes about crabs and skipping rocks at daybreak.

And there in the hollow is where Jay first proposed, and where I sat silently, stupidly, unable to say yes or no. When I thought about signing up for the long haul, I could imagine all the potential pleasures as well as the regrets, and I took this to mean I just wasn't the marrying kind. But I also thought that maybe someday, too late, I'd wake up to find that's exactly what I am. How can you make a decision for the rest of your life if you're not even sure you've yet become the person you'll always be? And is there even such a thing as the person you'll always be? Now I wonder if I will always be this: the person who never really answered the question at all but instead just ran into the freezing surf, joking how it's true what the locals say, that only tourists actually use the water.

For the funnymoon we camped for a week near Walden Pond and made day trips to Boston like we were tourists there. Jay had told Laura he was at a convention in Dallas, of all places. We spent a whole day shopping for the ten-gallon hat he'd promised to get her while he was away.

At the science museum he explained the Möbius strip, all curves and flips you can travel forever, a tricky and endless loop. At the Museum of Fine Arts we walked the Egyptian rooms—10 percent artifact and 90 percent plaster assembled into temples that no exact science could project.

Too early in May for tourists, we walked the clear ring of the pond, imagining the glaciers cleaving the earth to make way for that kidney-shape of water. "It's not too late," he said by Thoreau's old cabin. It's nearly requisite that each visit we talk about marriage, and we've gotten good at culling lines from anywhere. I told Jay that still water means not to rock the boat. He pointed out the mallards and how they mate for life. We swapped lines of graffiti that Boston's overeducated vandals had scrawled on the rocks.

He read, "Explore thyself."

I read, "A man is rich in proportion to the number of things he can afford to let alone."

One rock commanded: *Semper ubi sub ubi*—always where under where. At the time I thought that was very funny. I must
have conceived right there, near the birch trees and stones.

I've always thought of our relationship as the product of some
kind of enlightened decision. It's only right now, cheek against
the cold bathroom stall, that I wonder if all this driving and giggling and sneaking around has been anything but the greatest
effort not to decide.

"This is it, kid. Now what do I want? To forget the whole thing
and slip out of this wedding or to strut out to the dance floor and
storm the beach with Jay?"

Even over the running sink I can hear Laura's friends singing
along with the band. There is the murmur of celebration, the air
gone dizzy with music and glee. Out the window the small waves
lap to the shore, ankle high and endless, and you'd never guess
how cold. The mirror shows small nests of wrinkles at my eyes.
The paper towels at the washbasins are scripted with Laura's name
and Jay's and that splotch of jelly bean—a bright pink seed—a
promise of something sweet and hopeful and ready to hatch. It
always seemed like there was so much time. What ever happened
to all that time?

Back outside, the dance floor is teeming with some kind of
bustle, the rustle of taffeta, the clacking of heels. The bridesmaids
are diving for Laura's bouquet. "Mine," shouts one, giving Laura
a high five.

I find Drew by the buffet nibbling on cream puffs. "Drew?"
I ask. "Can I keep visiting here? Am I kidding myself or can I
still visit here?" I'm talking too fast and still clutching my used
towel, the pink print and blotted lipstick crumpled and squashed
like some tiny life form.

"Are you doing okay?" he asks.

The photographer takes pictures. Jay's mother waves to me.
Across the floor, Laura and Jay slow-dance. And the world un-
spins and backs away, the tight spool of it unwound into tangle
and mass. The only thing I've ever known is that it takes just
fourteen minutes on the pike before I miss him, and I never
wanted to give that up. It would be, I've always thought, a terrible mistake to go and give that up. How can you know more
than that? I never seem to know more than that.

When there's barely anyone left at the wedding, Drew scavenges a plastic bag from somewhere and fills it with all the jelly beans that are left. "What is this?" I ask. "Your bright idea of a consolation prize?"

"Happy birthday," he says. "You deserve something a little sweet for the road."

I've been invited to stay over just about everywhere but the bridal suite, but I've decided to turn thirty-three in the privacy of my own home.

"Congratulations." I give Laura an awkward hug. "Bye," she stretches out the word, half sorority farewell, half taunting catcall, as though it leaped out of her mouth before she could decide.

I want to take some pictures of the beach before leaving. There is a film of light hanging over the water, between the wedding and the horizon's deep blue.

"Let's go," Jay says, helping me with my jacket.

"Andrew, go with them," Laura pleads. She is toasted, lit, three sheets to the wind.

"Are you kidding?" Drew tells her. "I haven't had a dance with you yet." He navigates her out to the floor, a trail of ribbons and lace and her gurgling coo.

The ocean is a tangle, a drunken snit of a tantrum, the breakers far off, just wily ripples when they hit the sand. This beach isn't lush with dunes like the beaches of my youth, nor is it fluffy, white, and narrow like shores I've photographed. It is craggy and difficult, and also wide and calming. The sand is cold underfoot and stubbornly packed in place.

"Well, what'd you think?" Jay asks, and we sit on the rocks.

"It was good," I say. "I mean, I liked the candy after all."

I hold the camera high overhead so it will catch our shadows, which run long behind us on the wet, hard beach. "Here's a wedding picture for you," I tell him, setting the aperture wide to let in the light. I can imagine what we must look like from the bathroom window back at the banquet hall: Jay emphatically wedding-perfect in his black tuxedo; the browny beige of my dress getting lost against the sand.

"You know," he says, "half the time that I imagined this wedding, I thought it would be the thing to finally push you to the edge. I imagined you jumping up in the middle of the ceremony, or better yet, just raising your hand in this snide sort of way and saying, 'Who the hell are we kidding here,' and then we'd both run out together and drive to Disney or something."

There's heat lightning off in the distance, quick white flashes all sizzle and no sound. I've got one hand on my belly and one hand in Jay's. I am not thinking of the long, sleek stretch of I-95 that could get us to Orlando by this time tomorrow. I'm thinking that suddenly there's a part of my anatomy I can refer to as a womb. It was always just stomach, and now it's a womb.

"You know," I say, breathing in long and deep, enough air to scout out the right words and buoy them to the surface, "what I wish most sometimes is that I'd just gotten pregnant and everything would have gotten pushed to some choice. It wouldn't have been so easy to just come and go."

"God," he says. His eyes are wide and he starts a slow shake of his head. "I used to wish for that all the time."

My throat fills with something clunky, awkward, cold. I cough and Jay pats me on the back. He rubs my right shoulder and it occurs to me that this is the last time he'll rest the sure weight of his hand at the base of my neck or that he and I will sit together here on this beach. There is the horrible tug of tears at my eyes and throat, but I'm not sure whether to diagnose them as terror or relief. I don't know what to do, so I look all around—up and down, to Jay and away from him, to the shore and the sky and the night. How do you know? How do I know? It's only from so far in the future that you can see if you've done the right thing. Until then, it's pick and hold your breath. Pick, wait and see. Pick and that's that. That is that.

The trip home is bullet-fast and easy, all clear road and right mind. Look, I know it's something to sleep with the same person by your side every night, sheets worn in two strips from the anchors of bodies. And there must be a certain comfort in someone knowing all the colds behind the pills in your medicine chest. But maybe it's just this I like—my quick steps in a beach parking lot and a secret shout of *I love you* into the night. Maybe I just love the car that starts at the turn of my key and the fact that I never have to adjust the seat. Or maybe I love the hills that arch and buckle beside me and that I could pull over on a whim to lie down and watch the sky. Maybe there's something spelled out in the stars, something like: *Hold out — there's good stuff waiting ahead.*

Or maybe it's all for this unforeseen moment: when I get to the Mobil on I-95, there's a bunch of flowers in a styrofoam cup on top of the trash. From the pump I can't see if they're immersed in water, a sign of a conscious gesture, or if the cup got abandoned first and then casually filled, discarded flowers from a torn love affair, the bemused redecoration of some window-box robber. Here I am, barefoot and pregnant, beige shoes in the backseat, but all I can do is walk over to check. There is water in the cup, clear and fresh, like those flowers were set out moments ago just for me, a holy high-five from the fates come in the form of baby's breath and peonies. As I fill up the tank, I lean back against my car to get a good look at the crowded New England night sky. I have to admit, I can feel that birthday kind of excitement coming on. And before getting back on the road, I take the bouquet, a prize it seems, for finally leaving indecision behind.

The Dumpling King

Caleb had made no plans for his thirty-first birthday, nonevent that it was. Who needed the involved beach outings of his teens or the raucous barbecues of his twenties? Who needed the multikeg spectacle of his big three-o? But when he awoke on the summer Saturday marking his birth, the prospect of spending a quiet day at home did not leave him feeling well adjusted and mature as he'd anticipated—oh, to the contrary. For one thing, there was the discomforting fact of the cat hairs that still hovered around him in the morning light, the relentless ghost of the cat he and his girlfriend of three years had bought together, the cat that had moved out with Daphne nearly ten months ago.

There was also the embarrassing fact that after nine swelter-
ing summers in his Brooklyn apartment Caleb still hadn't kicked
down the cash for an air conditioner. The place was so hot it always smelled like corn muffins baking. Nearly a decade after college, and he was still relying on ice pops and marijuana to get
himself through July.

Caleb adjusted the box fan in the window, stealing a look
through the spinning blades, his own street flickering before
him like a film. Just last year the city had lined his block with
spindly trees, shaky as foals in their boxed-off beds, quivering
with every passing car like an animal scared and unable to move
on. If he didn't get out of the house soon he'd get stuck in a dis-
quieting contemplation of the real estate, the relationship, the career, or the cash that might mark his adulthood. If he didn't get
out of the house there'd be no avoiding the birthday phone call
from his mom.

And so, at this eleventh hour, Caleb decided to throw himself a party after all. By noon he'd made arrangements to bor-
row a friend's swanky Tribeca apartment for the occasion and he
scrambled to properly put out the word, leaving a flurry of phone
messages all over town. Then, finally, he got the hell out of the
house.

He felt better as soon as he arrived in Chinatown, surrounded
by crowds and moving with purpose through the narrow streets.
He pressed past storefront tables tangled with knobs of ginseng
root. He snaked around an impromptu vending table piled high
with women's underwear by stepping into the wet gutter, hopping a pile of brownish ice. As he navigated his way, he imagined
being watched all the while—by Daphne or an old friend from
home, someone who would note the confidence of his stride, his
ease with this elaborate route. He had grown up in Brunswick,
Maine, and he took a certain pride in having developed a little
New York expertise—discovering for himself the flower and fish
markets, the hidden record stores on Avenue C, which hotels to
pop into when he had to use the john. And there was this, his latest find, The Dumpling King.

He descended into the tiny basement storefront, the small space abuzz with fluorescent lighting that kicked up a green hue off the cracked linoleum floors. Refrigerated cases lined each wall, each filled with bags of frozen dumplings—made on the premises—meant to be steamed or fried. They were packaged in plastic bags as big as bed pillows and marked with ingredients stickers spelled out in Chinese. Sometimes there was no bigger relief than finding himself off the hook from having to communicate with the world. The air conditioner was on full blast, and Caleb took a moment to enjoy it, leaning back to press his shoulders and neck against one of the cool glass doors.

He then moved quickly through the store, releasing puffs of frosty air at his face as he opened each case, selecting bag after bag. He wasn't sure which symbols corresponded to which fillings, but he identified each bag with a whisper: "shrimp, pork, chicken, veggie," as if saying the word alone would make it so. There were so many dumplings he'd have to put a pot on every burner. The kitchen would be bubbling and steamy, and he would scatter the living room with heaping platters and bowls, everyone wanting to know where he'd found such delights.

He selected his favorite sauces from a shelf behind the counter: oyster, soy, pepper, and tamarind seed oil. The cashier wrapped the bottles and jars in paper, and Caleb put them into his knapsack. Then he watched as the man bound the frozen bags together with twine. This, Caleb had no choice but to carry between his arms like a large sack of laundry. He could feel the cold dumplings rubbing through the plastic, making—he was sure—the insides of his arms splotch with shades of pink and purple. Later he might, joke about how he'd carried this bulk of bounty all day and these were his war wounds, these brief little smudges of glory.

He walked west briskly, with an eye out for a cab, and it was then, at the corner of Church and Canal, that he spotted Daphne's small thin frame. She was stepping out of her decade-old Chevy Blazer, so enormous a vehicle it was astounding she'd managed to park it on the same streets that normally lacked space enough for a compact.

There were women all around the streets and Caleb suddenly noticed them—women in heeled boots and in tight black pants; women with shiny sheets of blonde hair in a broad stripe down the back. There were women with painted nails and with hand-bags; women with cigarettes who moved with a confidence that scared him.

And there was Daphne. She stood before the parking meter dig-ging into her jeans pockets, extracting quarters, turning the dial. Caleb laughed; she was so little. He was a big guy, tall and a little bulky, especially in winter in the L.L.Bean sweaters his mother continued to send. And Daphne, by contrast, had to keep a ratty pillow in her front seat just so she could see over the hood.

Caleb followed Daphne at a distance, her red ponytail bobbing before him like a carrot. After some deliberation, he'd included her in this morning's invitations, in part because she still wanted to be friends and in part because he was pretty sure she would show. He wanted a crowd despite the late notice; truth be told, volume tended to work on him like a salve. He wondered if she had gotten his message, was coming to his party, if that's why she was downtown today defying the odds of finding a place to park.

She turned off of the bustling main drag and heaved open the door of a small boutique. Caleb stopped in front of the spare, gray window displaying white dresses hung like marionettes from nylon line. Beyond, the store's ceilings rose cathedral-like. Caleb could see two rows of clothing rods hanging from the ceiling on thick burlap straps. Another woman entered the store and the cascading dresses caught air and billowed, then dropped abruptly, like modern dancers, with the closing of the door. He imagined the fine hairs of Daphne's profile lifting and dropping. He missed her suddenly very much. Was she buying, he wondered, some-thing to wear to his party?

She had disappeared into a large tented dressing room, the beige curtains tumbling in excess to the floor. A woman with blonde braids used a special pole to bring a dress down from one of the hanging rods. Anchored atop the high pole and parading toward him down the center aisle of the store, the long white dress came into focus for Caleb, as if he'd finally discerned the form in an optical illusion that had seemed, at first, just a wash of colors—these were wedding dresses. He shifted the big cold bundle in his arms, the plastic tugging on his perspiring skin.

Was Daphne getting married? Caleb's face flushed and his head felt light. Daphne would still call occasionally, and he would give in to playful conversations—they would laugh!—and when he hung up the phone he'd feel a strange mix of pleasure and regret. But still, he could hate her, he could.

The curtain shifted and out stepped Daphne, still in her jeans and holding the fabric open for her best friend, Lindsay, a long white trail following her out of the dressing room. Of course it was Lindsay. Caleb stepped into the store, the opening door stirring enough breeze to flutter the train as Daphne and the braid lady knelt around Lindsay in the dress.

"Daphne," he said, suddenly self-conscious about his red high-tops and his baggy shorts, his plastic-wrapped bundle, the heap of meat fillings thawing in this store. "I saw the Blazer parked on the street and this is the first window I peeked in and here you are."

"Hi, Caleb," Lindsay said, laughing in a giddy combination of self-consciousness and glee. "I'm getting married."

"I see that," Caleb laughed also. "And I've got all these dumplings." He scratched at his neck, aware that Daphne hadn't yet spoken. There were streaks of blonde mixed in with her red hair and he wondered if she'd had something done or if she'd spent the last month outside, maybe playing tennis or hanging out with new friends at the beach.

Daphne removed a few pins she had been holding between her lips. She kept them in one hand and held Lindsay's hem tight in the other. "Happy Birthday," she said.

"You got my message? That I'm having a party?"

She nodded. "I'll be there. I'll come by a little later."

Of course she would. When they saw each other last month for a drink, he'd found himself irritated at how willing she seemed to get back together and how longingly she looked at him across the table, how nervously she'd sat peeling the label from her beer.

They both were still and silent for a moment, Daphne holding the wedding dress hem and Caleb insulated with his big bale of dumplings, and it felt to Caleb like the stage was set once again for their familiar war. A couple entered the store and Caleb watched the hanging dresses fill with air and billow, rounding out like maternity wear. Good god.

"I should get going," he said, though neither girl responded.

They had turned their attention back to the dress, the triptych of Lindsay's image in the hinged mirror like a small bridal army.

———

Caleb's best friend, Ed, had recently moved with his wife into a swanky apartment in Tribeca. The couple had been heading out of town when Caleb called this morning, but they'd emphatically offered up their space. It was high-ceilinged and airy, with a view striking enough to keep even the natives dazzled for a while, and since it was easy to get to, people could stop by even if they'd already made other plans.

Caleb picked up the keys from the doorman, nodding politely over his bundle. He let himself into the apartment and stood for a while in the bay of the floor-to-ceiling windows. Straight ahead, he could see the red-bellied McAllister tugs plugging along the river. He could just make out the numbers on the backs of buses that passed far below, and the moment the four digits came into focus, he felt like he might be heading into a free fall right over Manhattan. It was almost too much to imagine living this way. What exactly, he wondered, did one have to give up in order to live this way?

———

In honor of the party, Caleb had hung a string of small red lights across the windows, gratuitously decorating an already glimmering skyline. Despite the late notice, Caleb had drawn together quite a crowd. He knew a lot of people in New York. He had friends from college at NYU and friends from Maine who had also moved to the city. He knew people from bars and clubs and from the various jobs he'd had—most recently at the ad agency jingle house on Twenty-Eighth Street, where, for the good grace of health insurance, he'd been working for the last year coming up with lyrics that rhymed things like *cola* and *rock 'n' roller*.

By eleven o'clock the place was buzzing with friends and acquaintances offering kisses on the cheek and last-minute gifts, the best the corner store had to offer: a six-pack of beer, a bouquet of flowers, bubblegum cigars. But despite the dress pants and short strappy dresses worn by the faction of the group heading off later for fancier fare, everyone gathered on the floor around Ed's low coffee table to pick eagerly from the blue and green ceramic bowls full of dumplings and dipping sauces.

Caleb told stories about his job and his neighborhood; what he lacked in stability he made up for in anecdote and he loved to perform. His friends laughed, reaching for dumplings to dip, ashing cigarettes in nearly empty sauce bowls, the wet embers emitting a satisfied hiss. He told of his upstairs neighbor, the lonely-but-loving deli clerk. "He brings home the vats of salads that are too old to sell. The macaroni. The coleslaw. He has so many salads they won't even fit in his fridge, so he divvies them up into Tupperware to leave on the doorstep of every apartment." Caleb looked around at his small, rapt audience. "Then he spends the whole evening out on the stoop, Mr. Congeniality, passing out spoons, saying, 'Go eat, people. Eat quick!' "

And then, just as concentration broke, just as purses were gathered and jackets extracted from the other room, in walked Daphne, making her way through the distracted crowd toward him. She was wide-eyed and windblown; she must have parked a mile away. Leave it to her to miss everything good. He watched a scrap of dumpling skin float between cigarette butts in the soy sauce; a tall girl put on her jacket and lifted her long hair out from under the collar; someone tossed a pack of Winstons in a crumple to the floor.

"Happy Birthday, Caleb," Daphne said in her scratch of a voice. She brought a hand to her face, tucked a red wisp of hair behind her ear. An unfamiliar silver bracelet rolled over the delicate bone of her wrist. "I'm sorry I'm late."

"Oh, Daphne!"

"Hi, Daphne!"

Caleb watched the bustle of hugs. "Where are you going? Where's everyone going?" Daphne asked.

"The Brooklyn Bridge. There's a party at the base of it. You can come along."

Daphne made a show of rolling up her sweatshirt sleeve, dusting off her jeans. "I don't think so," she said. "What are you doing, Caleb?"

"More of this," he sat back on the cool leather couch. He was wearing a nice new shirt and it felt good on his skin. He toasted his beer to the room. "There might be more people swinging by."

He watched Daphne survey the scene, hesitate, then find a beer. The crowd left in two big packs, their murmur fading down the hall.

"I've come empty-handed," Daphne admitted, without any real apology. "I've had quite a day as dressmaker. We just finished about an hour ago."

"You tired?"

"You have no idea." Daphne rolled her head in a woozy way and took a determined drink from her beer.

Caleb looked at the clock on the VCR and tried to imagine who else might be coming. Everyone was gone and it wasn't even midnight. They sat for a moment in silence. These days, being near Daphne made him feel disoriented, as though he'd been living inside her for the last three years and was finally free to just take in the view. Sometimes he wondered about things like how much time they'd spent together cumulatively in different activities: eating, for example, or kissing or laughing, or the amount of time he'd spent waiting for her at public rest rooms. It was impossible to guess. "It's hot in here, isn't it?" he said.

She bit at her lip. "A little."

Caleb eyed the mess of plates and clutter, the soggy remnants of a party Daphne hadn't witnessed. In truth, he couldn't think of anyone else who might be coming; there was just himself and Daphne and all this debris. What they should do to salvage the evening, he thought, was to leave the mess and head out once again, this time for the wide-open spectacle of the roof.

Up thirty stories, Caleb and Daphne straddled the building ledge, facing each other like two friends on a seesaw, each with a leg dangling out over the city. There was an odd composite of the Manhattan skyline around them. They could see the Supreme Court building with its short steps and broad columns, and the East River in the distance, which caught the lights of Brooklyn in its current. The sky was a smoky gray that would have looked black anywhere but in the city.

"So have you been dating?" she asked.

"A little. You?"

"Not really. They opened up a new market near me and it's like a debutante ball. I get propositioned by the butcher, the baker, the whole bit. I like being asked but I don't know about going." She rolled her eyes.

"Ed and his wife keep setting me up on dates. She's got about a hundred cousins and they all look exactly the same. They're like some science fiction army."

He hated going on the dates. He had no idea what to talk about anymore. How many winning first dates had he spent in his twenties sitting around over a beer and thinking up ridiculous band names! But at thirty, he found that desirability had morphed into something else. They'd changed the game on him suddenly, and now he was behind.

"Enough about dating," Daphne said, inspecting a small cut on the back of her hand. "Did you get anything good for your special day?"

"People brought things. And you know my mother always goes over the top." Caleb shrugged. "She's actually coming to visit in a couple of weeks. She's actually going to stay at my place."

"That's something."

Caleb imagined leading his mom up the steep, narrow steps of his building, eyeing his tired, hand-me-down furniture. He used to have three guys from school as roommates, but there had been a steady attrition. Caleb alone had held on to the lease.

"I know what you're thinking," he said. "That she'll finally get me to move home."

"I'm not thinking anything. You may be thinking that, but I'm not."

"So do you want to meet her? You should meet her," he said. In three years he'd kept the two deliberately apart, though now their meeting was something he almost craved.

Daphne didn't answer. She just took a drink from the beer that rested between them and hopped back onto the roof. She walked to the other side of the water tower, her bright white sneakers nearly glowing white along with the pigeon droppings.

"What is that?" she asked, pointing to a building one block farther west. It was tall, with no windows, no markings or identification, just a huge rectangle of bricks yielding no clue as to what went on inside it.

"I heard it's a power plant. Or maybe the phone company owns it. I forget," he said. She looked so separate from him all the way across the roof, like someone he only vaguely knew. He climbed down off the wall to join her. Together they surveyed the rest of the scene, the civic buildings, the small parks, the white-lit hole in the earth where the towers once stood.

"Maybe it's an urban prison," Daphne tried. "A drunk tank. Or some kind of holding cell."

"I am a drunk tank," Caleb said, holding his arms out, and rather than resting his fists on his hips, he let his bent arms dangle, hanging awkwardly down. The gray sky over the river looked icy, as though he should feel cold. The skin on his arms was goose-bumped, but he couldn't tell if it was just his skin or his whole self; how did he really feel? He had no idea.

"So do you want to maybe meet my mom?" he asked again.

"I don't know. I don't think so," Daphne said, kicking at the roof tar. "I can't believe that *now* you want me to meet your mom."

He could picture them all at a museum or something, the Botanical Gardens. His mother could finally see who was hanging out all that time, who was taking care. "Christ, can't you give an answer," he said. There were so many things he was glad to be free of—Daphne's hair elastics played like ring toss on his shampoo bottles; the way she'd get very quiet during wedding scenes in movies, keeping her head straight toward the screen, as though letting Caleb know he was under no pressure. He knew her so well.

He lunged forward and grabbed at her, unsure whether he was about to hug her or spin her in some sort of dance move, but he tripped and stumbled, her small sneakers tangling between his legs. Together they fell to the black, dusty surface of the roof.

"Ouch." Daphne squirmed out from beneath him. "Oh. I think I have glass in my hand," She knelt and held her left hand in her right, angling it in an effort to catch light.

Caleb knelt too, facing Daphne, making them look like two grown people about to dance at half height. He took her left hand in his, rotating it in front of him. It was an amazing tiny thing. It was so small and exact—a perfectly hand-shaped hand. Her palm was black from the soot, but the pale, clean spaces between her fingers shone, highlighting the outline of the form. These were the hands that had touched him everywhere. There was one time his eyelash had grown into his eye. He could hardly see. He remembered how he'd even let her touch his eye.

He ran his thumb over Daphne's palm and she let out a brief moan. He dribbled some beer onto her hands and he rubbed them together, trying to get them clean. "Don't," she said. "Ouch."

Other than that, the whole city was quiet, without sirens and horns and the backfire of trucks, just her hand in his, small, warm, and perfect.

"Caleb?" she said lightly, questioning him, the same small voice she used to use in the middle of the night, making sure, even in sleep, that he was there and everything was all right.

He didn't know what to say. "I can't believe you won't come and meet my mom."

"I should go downstairs. I should get this cleaned off and go home. I have to meet Lindsay again tomorrow at ten."

"Don't be dramatic." God, he really didn't want her to leave. "You're fine," he said, though he could, in fact, see a swollen mark on the heel of her hand, pierced by a sliver that caught light. He rubbed his thumb across it. If he pressed hard on the glass he could make her bleed.

Daphne shook her head—like a stubborn and refusing baby, as if shaking her head like that might keep her from crying. "This is the fight," she said. "This is the same fight we always have. You can surround yourself with every doting jackass you've ever met, but I'm the only one you like more the less I like you." He watched her face as she said it, the way her small eyes were pinched and piercing, as though she thought she could see right through him—through his parties and friends, through his skin and his skull, to the very core of his littlest fears, all the truths about him as simple and plain as cake.

She tried to pull her hand away. "Come on. I have to go."

He didn't know exactly what he wanted, except, he thought, to make her cry. If she was going to leave, he wanted her bawling. Caleb could see black marks smudging the inseams of her pants from when they sat on the ledge. She had the same soot on her shirt and her face. She pulled up a sleeve to inspect her elbow. He wished they hadn't broken up, or that they hadn't broken up *yet*, that he could break up with her all over again now.

"Look at you," he said. "You're just this little fucking ticking clock." She was so small, he thought, the city so large, so much his own. He knew it so well! He could lift Daphne up in a heartbeat and send her soaring out over the edge. He imagined spinning himself in a circle, Daphne's small bony ass resting in his palm like a shot-put. He could launch her—he could—over the roofs and the parks, past the courts and the traffic, maybe even clear through the windshield of her own ludicrous car.

He could do it, he knew, probably even with one hand. He tilted his head all the way back, arching his neck, anxious for day. He wanted the sky to turn silvery and then light. He wanted to feel some bit of heat on his face.

And
Then
You
Stand
Up

It was spring break. Francie's students were off to Daytona Beach on the annual Pilgrimage to Paradise, the product of tireless fund-raising and a Web-savvy search for a cheap group rate. Francie, by contrast, would be spending the week in Boston, riding out the tail end of winter with her best friend and her best friend's daughter. Talk about diminishing expectations! "It's a pilgrimage for *hugs*," she explained to her students, who just shrugged and surged down the hallways, all hoots and hopefulness and the smell of Tropical Blend.

Francie took a red-eye from San Francisco to Boston and slept in a window seat doughy with Dramamine, waking up upon landing to a drizzly dawn. Now, Rita, her best friend, pulled up curb-side at Logan. "Get in! Get in!" she called to Francie out the pas-senger window, not offering hugs or even help with the luggage. Such a hurry, thought Francie, and for what?

"Breasts," Rita said. "It's unbelievable. I went in to check on Pauleen this morning and there they were, pressing through her nightshirt."

"What do you mean she has breasts?" In Francie's mind, Pauleen was still a lover of baseball cards, a kisser of dogs, all *child*—sexless and brave, ready to take on any roller coaster, risk any belly flop, write gushing letters to TV stars and expect letters in return. "She's only eleven; *I* barely have breasts yet."

"You'll laugh," said Rita, rushing through a yellow light. "She's suddenly a hundred feet tall and the entire world's a friendship bracelet—embroidery thread, hardware, fishing hooks."

"It's been too long," Francie sighed and looked out the window. The last time she had seen these Boston streets, it had been rain-ing and she'd been driving too fast. She actually found it fascinat-ing to think about: the car and all of its contents—the seats and the floor mats, the tape in the tape deck, and Francie behind the wheel— all of it going ninety. Then, there occurred the particu-lar and irreversible moment when Francie and a wayward deer happened to collide on the Massachusetts Turnpike. The impact killed the deer and set the car off course, but Francie herself con-tinued like a shot through the windshield, piercing the air some-where near Sturbridge, the arrow of her body led sixty feet by her eye. Always the underachiever—just a little more oomph and she could have crossed the state line!

She'd lost her left eye to the ordeal and gained a cross-hatching of scars from her face to her knee all along that side of her body. Such a sight she had been! At first, even strangers felt it appro-priate to ask what had happened—the wounds had been so fresh and raw, surely they would heal! But now, three years later, with the damage calmed and uniform in color, no one ever asked what had happened anymore. It was as if Francie were a woman sim-ply *meant* to have one side of her face mapped with scars, as if genetics had her earmarked to have a too-shiny glass eye lodged like a beetle in the center of a web. As soon as she could, Francie had moved to a small mountain town in northern California—a hippie town full of people with chosen hippie names, everyone trying to disappear.

Now, out the window, she noted that the streets were just as she'd left them. There was no flash of sun off the quaintly painted shutters, no warm, ruddy light off the brick sidewalks, no glint of dew on the bulbs just poking up from the flower beds. The street corners were still puddled and littered with broken umbrellas, as if it had been raining for the last three years, the stage waiting for Francie to step out and start over again.

"I've got to be honest," Francie said in the silence. "I'm a little nervous about Pauleen. What if I scare her?"

"You're not going to scare her," Rita said as she turned into her driveway, its smooth brown pebbles scraping together under the wheels. "And if she makes fun of you, you can make fun of her in return. It's official: You have my permission."

The front lawn was overhung by great oak branches, still bald but thick enough to shade without leaves, to give a sense of the umbrella they provided when in bloom. Rita's husband, Jim, was standing at the door with a cup of coffee in hand, tie waiting slack around his neck.

"I'm glad I caught you," he said between kisses on each of Francie's cheeks. "I have to be at work early to oversee the new interns who oversee the petri dishes. I'm the season's bacteria watchdog. Grrrr." Jim bared his teeth and left. He hated the lab, wanted to be an animal trainer.

"I made this for you!" exclaimed Pauleen, running out the door and down the steps in front of the house. She was in a T-shirt and sweats, barefoot on the slate. She was pretty, with big eyes, light hair, nice teeth. Francie anticipated the girl's hesitation, but Pauleen threw her arms around Francie's waist, and when she withdrew from the hug, she opened her palm to reveal a bracelet strung of wing nuts and beads. "My favorite colors." Pauleen explained. "All of them."

"Thanks, doll." Francie put her bag down on the ground between her feet, clasping the bracelet against her stomach to secure it with the other hand.

"I could make it longer if you'd rather have an anklet," Pauleen offered, already retreating into a hunch, reaching her fists inside her T-shirt hem to push it out, away from her body.

"No, no." Francie turned her wrist over for Pauleen's inspection. "This is great, this is fine. It's good to see you."

In the last few years Pauleen had grown at least half a foot. She was about five foot two, almost her mother's size. Pauleen had pulled her ashy hair off her face with one terry-cloth headband and used a second to tie up a ponytail.

"Why aren't you ready for school?" Rita asked.

"I'm sick." Pauleen turned her attention to her mother. She made her eyes wide and let her face go slack. "I don't know what it is, but one minute I feel perfectly fine, and the next, I'm about to fall over."

"Well get dressed," Rita said. Her hair was sporty and short, a peppery blonde. She had little gold earrings; she even *looked* like a mom. "We'll get you right to the doctor."

Pauleen slid her arms inside her shirt and crossed them over her chest, doing her best to keep herself secret. Francie could picture the girl inspecting herself behind a locked bathroom door, not daring to touch either tender new bump, as if, left alone, they might just go away—Pauleen, the able girl who was frighteningly good at Boggle; Pauleen the uninhibited, who'd spent not just Halloween but also the three days after dressed in face paint and yarn as broccoli and cheese.

Rita placed a hand on the back of Pauleen's neck, then on the side of her face. "You're a little warm," she sighed. "Why don't you get back in bed."

Pauleen nodded and headed quickly to the house, the empty sleeves flailing beside her. Rita turned to Francie and gestured to her own chest. "O-ver-night," she whispered. "Did it happen like that for you?"

The long hallway from the front door to the kitchen was lined with framed photos hanging against the striped wallpaper. There was Jim in a cap and gown, Pauleen on a horse, Rita and Francie in black and white on a spring-break trip to Yosemite at twenty-six, shortly before Pauleen was born. In the photo they stood close, eyes alight, brown heads of hair blending together, both smiling devilishly. Francie's square chin was cocked forward, as if ready to take a punch. In some ways, she thought, so little had changed.

"Shoot me, shoot me, please," she'd said just the other day to the student who had come to take her picture for the yearbook. He was rumpled and charming; his heavy camera swung from the strap bunched in his hand. His hands, she'd noticed, were broad and decorated in black felt-tip pen, the careful markings of new adolescent love: a heart, a guitar, a phone number, a name, Donna. The whole thing had made Francie suddenly sad and self-conscious; he probably assumed that she'd never been courted in her life. He took her picture, but he didn't really look at her—not really. She could hardly remember what it felt like to be seen. She held her chin up, her smile intact, as he advanced the film, focused, and shot, as the shutter opened and released.

Francie followed the line of Pauleen's class pictures—Ms. Sturm's class, Miss Ellery's, Mrs. McPhee's—Pauleen taller and taller along the way.

"I'm usually a stickler for attendance," Rita asserted in the kitchen. The two friends were seated at the oak breakfast table, which was covered in colorful, hand-braided placemats, the coffeepot on a trivet between them. "But I don't think it's awful to let her get her head around things for a day or two. Besides, you're here. We can run around, three girls."

"You're a good mom," Francie said. "I always knew you would be."

"Don't get dramatic on me. Just because you didn't have a kid at twenty-six doesn't make you barren."

"All I said is that I think you're a good mom. I never said I was barren."

"I just want you happy."

"I'm happy. I'm happy. Look, the worst my students have come up with is Web Face and Fly Eye. And the worst that happens in bed is that men fixate on one side of my body, one side of my face, one breast, one thigh, depending on whether they're into proving bravery or sensitivity and whether they're out to prove it to me or to themselves. I'm not saying I can't understand; I just retain it, that's all, who loves to the left and who to the right."

"How romantic." Rita looked away, as she always did when it seemed inarguable that Francie had fallen behind.

Francie knocked oddly on the wooden table, not out of superstition but self-consciousness. Lately it seemed crucial to her that someone real—someone who knew her when—come have a look, a parent poking into a bedroom to say, Yes, yes, Things seem in order here.

She wanted someone to check in on her apartment, her haunts, to sit in on her class. "Are you with me?" she would ask the room of round faces. She could mention Pompeii, Plymouth Rock, the Civil War, and her students would nod blankly, none of them— not one—seeming to know what she was talking about. She had been shaped, she felt sometimes, by a single moment in time and space when no one was watching at all.

"So, speaking of romance, last week I was at the library flipping through some European art magazine," Francie began, "and there was a four-page folio on the art of Hans Hallmundson."

"Hans!" she'd exclaimed—out loud, in public—at the sight of his picture, his shock of blond hair, the tired lines at his eyes. His name had skipped from her lips like the greeting of a forgiving child. He was real—there he was. She thought she'd imagined him sometimes. "He's in Reykjavík, still copper-casting, still fish in bow ties— that whole fish-as-business-Icelandic thing—but I guess he's really gaining recognition now."

There, thought Francie, she'd said it. She could admit she checked up on him. He'd been a visiting lecturer for a year at Emerson College, and he and Francie had, in truth, enjoyed a very regular little affair. It had been a perfectly pleasant and terminal thing. He would return to Iceland, to a fiancée; Francie had understood that from the start. She'd never been particularly sentimental, had always been a little suspicious of romance—the alleged panacea of it, the great leap of faith. Romance, Francie believed, was one of those things that could look terrific on other people, but on herself it felt gaudy and hackneyed, a ridiculous prom dress. She and Hans had been casual, no big deal.

Yet occasionally, all her resolution would fracture into something giddy-making and light. On a spring trip to Mexico at a volcanic lake, she'd dug her hand into the ashen bottom, pulled up a mound of soil, and in it, there had been a ruby—who knew from where? It winked against the darkness of the sand. "My girl!" Hans exclaimed, his blue eyes flecked with glory and wonder. It could seem, at times, tremendous like that, like the world was coughing up its very treasures for them.

There were those kinds of moments from time to time—those kinds of moments and the fact that everyone she knew was getting married; that Pauleen was nine and Rita was busy sewing name tags onto her shorts for camp; that Hans's fiancée sent him long letters on blue parchment sheets that Francie could never translate even if she'd tried.

And Francie hadn't wanted more really. She'd been in grad school, proud to claim an enlightened satisfaction with her own slice of Hans. But shortly before Hans was to leave the states, she'd pitched a fit over burgers and shakes, over nothing, over feeling shortchanged and small. Was it so unreasonable to stand up for yourself, to declare to the world that you wanted more? She could hear her mother's voice: *What took you so long to figure that one out?*

"How dare you!" Francie had exclaimed, throwing her burger down.

"But Francie," Hans had said in the singsong of his strained English. She'd wanted suddenly not the ring and the house and the whole gaudy future but the simple promise of waking up and knowing he'd be there. "But Francie," he'd tried to calm her. She'd never counted on him to find the right words. Why, suddenly, now? And it was then, in a moment not exactly her own, that Francie had turned on her heel, stormed to her car, and sailed through the windshield and over a small piece of Massachusetts.

It was such a stupid story. If only she'd started out ten seconds sooner or later. If only she hadn't gone to dinner at all. Or if only she hadn't been the kind of person to go speeding off without a seatbelt in the first place, or to settle for the crumbs of affection of an affianced man. *Put simply*, Rita had said at the time, *if only you'd made it to adulthood with a shred of self-esteem intact.* And now, here it was—in the mirror every single morning, the inescapable fact of an overdue and botched clamoring for love.

She could hardly make herself look.

Rita's kitchen felt suddenly too warm, full of copper pots and candlesticks, too many wedding gifts. There was a long list of emergency numbers taped to the fridge—in-laws, doctors, neighbors, and friends—a perfectly printed, ballpoint safety net. There were baskets heaped with produce and glass jars of hearty grains. And there, Francie noticed, was Pauleen at the top of the spiral staircase that rose from the pantry just behind Rita's back. She was sitting, tucked into a ball with both her knees and her arms pulled underneath her sweatshirt. She was just a face hovering over fabric like a finger puppet, wide-eyed and taking everything in. The sight of her dug a hollow in Francie's chest, as if it were Pauleen to whom Francie owed some sort of explanation. The girl was, after all, probably the closest Francie would ever come to having a daughter of her own.

Pauleen proclaimed that she was feeling better and they decided to head for Salem so she could make up a field trip she'd missed for a history project. Pauleen had dolled up a little for the outing and she smelled exactly the way Francie remembered eleven-year-old girls smelling: sticky sweet and fruity, with strawberry bubblegum, strawberry lip balm, strawberry shampoo.

It was a Friday, still before noon, and the roads out of town were roomy and quick. The ramp up to the Tobin Bridge, green and colossal, spiraled before them. "Is this right? This never seems right to me," Francie said as the ramp drew a long loop onto the highway, directing them back toward the industrial terrain of the city before moving forward and past it.

She eyed the steely water of the harbor to her right and the cars zipping past. "So what's your project on?" Francie asked Pauleen, forcing herself to gain focus, keeping her eye on the dash.

"Essex. I can pick anything about Essex County and talk about the value of remembering our own history."

"What are you thinking?"

"Witches."

"You can't just go to the gift shop," Rita warned Pauleen in the rearview mirror. "You can't just get the cauldron of candy. You've got to *actually* do the tour."

"I know," Pauleen rolled her eyes. "This land is your land, this land is my land," Pauleen began singing suddenly and then left off. She turned to make sure the lock was depressed and then leaned against the door to read *The Babysitters' Club*.

Salem lay just sixteen miles north of Boston, but Rita took the route that was slow and curvy, cutting through the suburbs that spread up from the city. They passed tremendous barnlike houses, the windows small and pinched in the boxy structures, reminding Francie of perplexed-looking children, children whose eyes seemed lost in the great space of the face. It was amazing, she thought, how the language of the eye was the same as the language of the galaxies: the globe, the medical term for the eyeball; the orbit, the bony socket that keeps the eyeball in place; the pupil, the body's black hole—everything seen left to swarm in the chaos of the body's deep space.

"Well, I spoke to my mother," Rita said. "She has a surgeon all picked out for you, the son of one of her cronies."

"For love or reconstructive surgery?"

"You're a real charmer," Rita said.

"I wish you'd leave me alone."

"I'm just suggesting you be open."

"I'm open. I'm open." The last man Francie brought home, up the tiny steps to her house had been a cop—a rookie. He'd doted on her scars, tongued his way along them. Brave man he was! He had kissed the many seams of her cheek before rolling over to sleep facing the wall. Francie had slipped out of bed to sit on the small deck of her cottage, giant redwoods closing in around her. High above she could see just a perfect circle of sky, as if she were looking out from inside a canon, ready to be launched at the glowing face of the moon. "Besides," she said to Rita now, "Are you trying to make me feel better or is this actually about you?"

The car was quiet for a moment, the peculiar kind of quiet Francie most often experienced when walking into the girls' bathroom at school and even the breeziest conversation would cease. Francie gave those teenage girls encouraging little smiles—how pathetic and kowtowing she could be!—as if seeking from them some moment of grace and tacit recognition that she was more like them than not, and had also once expected the world.

In the back seat Pauleen played with the window control, sealing off and letting in quick bursts of cold air. "You should move here," she said.

Francie looked out the window to the gazebo on a Main Street green where a woman was bandaging the beams with purple ribbon and securing it in place with a staple gun.

"Maybe." Francie doodled with her finger in the felt of the front seat, drawing and undrawing the same concentric circles, turning them outward, and turning them in.

It was hazy in Salem, the streets empty and parking plentiful. Rita picked up a map at the visitors' center and passed it to Francie. "Guide us."

Francie breathed deeply and closed her eyes. She absorbed calm, swelled with it, as if it were humidity. "Do you know what they call the painted red line on the sidewalk?" read Francie from the map. "The Heritage Trail. The great Heritage Trail of Essex County links two wax museums and a pirate memorial, among other attractions."

"What's that, then?" Pauleen pointed to the green witch painted in the street.

Francie checked the map, "That's just where you get the mini-mall shuttle."

At the Salem Witch Museum they took a tour of the wax reenactments chronicling the witch trials of 1692. Along with a scattering of others, Francie, Rita, and Pauleen gathered around a nine-foot circle which was inscribed with the names of the dead and glowed red on the floor, like a portal to hell the size of a kiddie pool. There were thirteen dioramas representing the afflicted young girls—life-size! in wax!—frozen in time forever at their worst, writhing and wild-haired.

"Why are they doing that?" asked Pauleen.

"Let's see," Francie consulted the plaque on the wall. "Their behavior was attributed to either one of two things—ergot poisoning or simply being girls."

A voice-over echoed through the museum, playing through speakers crackling with dust, a menacing narration of facts. Spotlights flashed in chaos around the room, highlighting the seizures and stutters of the accused. A sound track played the clap of thunder, the baying of dogs, the stiff iron slam of locked prison bars.

"Questions? Comments?" asked the witch-museum guide. She was about twenty-four by Francie's guess, with jet black hair, a signet ring, and a silver skull dangling around her neck on a chain.

"Was everyone hanged?" Pauleen asked.

"Almost everyone." The guide gestured with an open palm, revealing a pentagram tattooed on the inside of her wrist. "One of the accused was just pressed to death, taken out to fields and blanketed in rocks."

Francie imagined the cold stones on her face, the weight on her gut. She imagined her muscles contracting for as long as they could before giving out, collapsing under the mass. She imagined low, pained moans barely surfacing in the mist and all the people gathered to listen and watch until finally leaving the airless body alone. Francie stared at the glowing red circle beneath her until it fell out of focus and her feet began to drown in the wash of color. She looked up to catch Pauleen staring at the ruined part of her face, following the scars with her eyes—Francie was sure— though it must have been too dark to see. It must have been.

When they stepped out of the museum, it was pouring. Rain was coming down in sheets too thick to drive through. Rita was suddenly nervous and thinking ahead, arranging the change in plans the new weather demanded. She had to check the sunroof, put money in the meter, and call Jim to say they'd be late getting back. She had always been unfailingly responsible.

"Why don't we go here?" said Pauleen, stopping in front of the Witch's Pot, a storefront full of ceramics, a clumsy circus of clay animals marching around a clay cauldron. She took Francie by the hand and looked at her intently. "We can make pottery. We can talk."

They sat at a muddy-looking picnic table in a chilly, fluorescent-lit room. They were rolling hunks of clay into balls and then slamming them down onto the clay boards, ridding the masses of air bubbles and killing time until they felt confident enough to begin. "I might make a lidded pinch-pot," Francie said, "You know, like they teach you in third grade."

Pauleen looked at her dumbly. Francie had recently read at the library that time really did move faster as you got older. It wasn't an illusion; the nervous system changed with age, speeding your interior clock, and there was no way of knowing if it was in synch with anyone else's. There was no way of having anyone catch up. "So," Pauleen said. "Can I ask you things?"

"Sex things?" Francie joked. "Boy things?" The last time Francie had been alone with Pauleen was years ago, babysitting—a night of hair braiding, long division, and snacks.

"About you," Pauleen said easily, "You things."

Francie grabbed a clay knife from the center of the table and began slicing bits off her slab. "You can ask me anything—about the accident or my eye. You shouldn't have to sit there and try to be polite. You're allowed to be curious. You might even learn something."

Pauleen picked up her clay pad and dropped it back onto the board, picked it up again and dropped it onto its other side, lazily sculpting it into a rectangle and then mashing it flat with her fist again.

"Does the fake eye hurt, like if you get something in it?"

"No," said Francie shaking her head. "I can feel the irritant under my lid, but it doesn't burn or anything like that anymore."

"Can you feel it? I mean, the glass. Is it cold?"

"Sometimes I can feel it, but only like an ache." She lumped her clay back together and began to roll it flat with a pin. "Mostly if I feel it, it's just when I'm thinking about it—about the accident really—and then I can feel it in my teeth. I sort of salivate, like with nails on a blackboard."

"Oh," Pauleen said softly. "What about the accident? Do you remember it?"

Francie sat still for a moment and took a breath, bringing her hands to her lap before realizing she was dirtying her skirt. Instead she picked up the clay knife again and began cutting out the letters of her name.

"I remember it the same way every time I think about it, but I know I'm not remembering anything real. Like I remember rocketing forward—not the impact but right before—soaring toward this big, sad moose face; big, sad eyes and the fur on his face hanging in these wet little triangles from the rain."

"But I thought it was a deer, right? Didn't you hit a deer."

"Right. This is just how I always remember it." She looked at Pauleen, her big careful eyes. "I remember flying by the sad, wet moose and then I just tuck and roll. You do gymnastics. You know how you have to tuck your chin to your chest so you can roll?" *Are you with me?*

Pauleen nodded.

"You know how you feel the mat at each point on your body— the back of your neck, your shoulders, down along your spine, and then at your tail bone, and then you stand up on your feet. Well, I remember the tuck and then rolling out at the hospital. But if I get tired I'll recall the moose, and the trajectory, the snap of the tuck, and then I feel like I'm rolling out wherever I am—at school the other morning, at the video store,' at the supermarket, like I just rolled out one-eyed in produce."

It was always catching up with her somehow, the accident, delivering her to any present moment. "Or right here," she told Pauleen. "It's like I just soared by the moose and landed talking to you. Like nothing else—not a single thing—has happened since then."

It always came as a raw shock, wresting her out of any pleasant day. This was her life. She kept watching it happen, looking on from the side. She'd recall, in panic, the most shameful things. She had, for a moment, truly enjoyed the drama. (She'd turned on her heel; stormed to her car! Had she been so ridiculous as to have felt a little like a movie star?) Then she'd feel a hot flash of something and be right back in the crash, emerging yet again as disoriented and meek, not quite herself and failed.

Pauleen had rolled her clay long and thin and then coiled it, rolling it along with the story, giving herself a visual aid, giving herself something to look at, as though she was afraid to look up. "I woke up with boobs this morning," she offered. "I swear to god I did."

Pauleen kept her eyes on her clay for a moment before lifting off her sweatshirt and reaching one arm behind her to grab at the back of the T-shirt she had on underneath. Her forearm was covered halfway up with threads, hardware, and beads. Her glitter nail polish glinted as she yanked at the fabric so it pulled taut against her brand-new breasts, which were two-tiered and as obvious as new tattoos—two small mounds, like patio anthills, each capped with a swollen nub. She began to laugh, an embarrassed defensive cackle. "They hurt."

"That'll stop. That'll go away."

"Don't tell Mom yet," Pauleen said, startling Francie with her new face of shame.

"I won't."

"Hey you're crying," Pauleen whispered, looking up.

Francie nodded.

"It still comes out both eyes," Pauleen said, naked in her fascination, letting her new breasts press against her shirt as she leaned closer.

Francie pushed her hair back before dropping her hands in her lap, sitting perfectly still to let the girl look. She knew exactly what Pauleen was seeing. The first few tears traveled left across the web, then diagonally down, and then right. When those deepest lines filled, they overflowed to shallower scars, until the rivulets traversed in all ways the jagged ruts of her face. She often wondered if the scars would grow deeper, like the Grand Canyon, salt and motion eroding the left side of her to the bone. Pauline pressed her small fingers at Francie's face. Francie could picture the clay from the girl's fingertips running like silt down her skin.

Finally, Pauleen slid her thin arms around Francie's neck, her slick ponytail sticking to the wet spots on Francie's cheek. Francie pulled the girl close, hands pressed on her back. She could feel Pauleen's ribs and tendons, her long thin muscles, shifting catlike under her skin. Francie inhaled, a great deep breath, her lungs light and elastic, infused with the potion of girlish smells—the promise of fresh grass, sea breeze, clean cotton, sweet fruit. "We will be fine," Pauleen said.

When Rita returned, Francie and Pauleen were sitting on the bench by the front door. They had their coats back on and they'd already washed their hands and paid, all the evidence of their activity gone, like lovers returned from a rendezvous.

For lunch, they had steamers and chowder at Pickering Wharf and then stood in the drizzle skipping French fries across the water and out to the gulls. They watched the fishermen bring in their dilapidated boats, emptying nets of wriggling cod. Francie could hear the fish slapping against the decks. Pauleen slouched beside her and started to hum, *This land is your land, this land is my land.* What if, Francie wondered, she had soared past the wet moose, given it a wink, and then tucked and rolled out here. "I could do this all day," she said to her friends, "We should do this all day."

Our
Little
Lone
Star

The radio announcer recited tornado warnings for the following counties: Travis, Washington, Gonzales, Gillespie. Terrific—except Audrey had no idea where in Texas she was. Was outside Houston a county? All she knew was that she was sixty-two years old, driving alone from New Jersey to Arizona to bring her daughter a car at college, and now, here was the terrorizing storm her husband had guaranteed.

She watched the horizon turn a faint toxic yellow, then darken to green and go black. All at once, the bright red truck ahead of her seemed to vanish in rain; gobs of it spat across the windshield. If her husband, Dan, were with her he'd already be rushing to an emergency shelter, somewhere underground with

Danish, and scratchy blankets, and local authorities on bullhorns. Her daughter, Molly, on the other hand, would be joyfully shoeless, skipping through puddles on the shoulder. Audrey herself wasn't sure what to do.

Was everybody getting off the road? Was anybody? Audrey squinted and leaned and tried to see, but it was impossible. The thunder grew deeper, seeming to emanate from the center of the earth and move skyward right through her. As slivers of lightning bisected the sky, Audrey realized that the cars around her had slowed to a crawl, that the lines on the road had disappeared, and even the trucks—the hearty trucks—were heading for the right lane. She was pressing her luck now, she knew.

But there before her were the golden arches, the first concrete thing she'd been able to discern in miles, so she made her way off the road. My savior, she laughed, Ronald McDonald. Truth be told, she was enjoying herself, finally.

She pulled into a spot marked Customers Only and made a dash for the restaurant, hopping puddles in the pitted lot. Inside, she rolled up her wet cuffs, bought hash browns and a Diet Coke, and chose the table littered with USA Today. From her seat she could see the whole parking lot. She watched the planes of rain twist around themselves, like sheets in a tangle, like a dog chasing its tail. Rain popped off the window and then fell away from it. It was erratic and unfollowable, like experimental music, like nothing she'd heard before.

"It's unreal!" She turned, delighted, to the man at the next table. He looked up from a stack of papers to stare at the weather, the puzzle of water and wind.

"It's weather." He drummed his tan hands on the table and his wedding ring clicked on the formica. "And it passes."

He was probably forty, maybe younger. He was freckled and tanned with years of sun.

"So, clearly you think it's the right thing, in rain like this, to get off the road?" Audrey looked at him hopefully. She wanted to hear that she was doing it right, behaving in a manner the rest of the world would consider reasonable. Even alone, she was still steeped with her husband's warnings; he had cautioned her about lightning, breakdowns, and car-jacking schemes. He had worked a long career in insurance and had developed a nearly devout faith in disaster, a deep belief in an inextricable link between calamity and pleasure. He'd shake his head in disgust at anything, even young marrieds in the market with party mix and a twelve-pack of beer. She'd hate to be overreacting. "Or am I just being wimpy?"

"I don't see anything wimpy about stopping in for a hash brown if you want one," he said.

"No, I guess there's nothing wimpy about that." She looked down shyly. She knew she didn't look sixty. For most of her life she had looked somewhat older than she was, but soon after fifty, with the exception of her hands, she had seemed to stop aging. She kept her hair a rich brown and wore it off her face, with bright scarves and headbands as though it were still the early sixties. This is my mother, Molly would joke, Gidget. Audrey was small and thin and had worn jeans and little loafers ever since she'd started the trip.

"Where are you from?" he wanted to know. Perhaps he thought she might be from somewhere specific, or perhaps it was just clear she wasn't from there.

"New Jersey," she said. "But not originally. Originally New York. The city."

"Well, I like that: loyalty." He started to laugh as though he'd reminded himself of something terrifically funny. There was something easy about his manner, the steady shift of his gestures, as if a sway moved ever through him. "And what brings you here? The Great Texas Beanie Baby giveaway?"

She was confused for a moment, but then she noticed that the windows were trimmed with the bright small dolls—little lobsters, roosters, ducks—modern-day wampum. "Oh yes, the Beanie Babies. And that I'm bringing a car to my daughter in Arizona. She's in college there, a junior. So I'm just passing through."

She felt relieved. She had always been good with strangers. She was always nervous on her own, riddled with doubts, until she ran up against the world and was reminded of how well she could do with it.

"And now it's raining on your parade. How very un-Texas in hospitality."

"It's true," Audrey said. "I was hoping for better."

"Well, that's a wonderful trip ahead of you." The stranger looked up from his coffee and nodded encouragingly.

"I know." She knew it would be a wonderful trip—though making the decision to go had nearly torn her apart. "My husband, Dan, had no interest in doing the drive. He wanted to ship the car out on a flatbed truck, but my daughter was adamantly against that. At twenty years old, she thinks I ought to live little."

Since she began college, Molly was so often righteous, armed with Women's Studies 101: *Are you going to spend your whole life locked in a house? C'mon mom. I cannot even relate to you at all.* But Molly's disappointment had accumulated in Audrey. She hated to be bullied, but she was afraid of alienating her daughter completely, her spirited girl, her only child.

"I'm just going to go," Audrey said finally and calmly to her husband. She might have taken his hand if she'd been standing closer, but he was walking back and forth, gathering his shirts in a neat stack for the dry cleaner's, his distraction itself a kind of dare. "Two weeks," she had said. "I'll be back in two weeks."

She had gone about her preparations with single-mindedness and silence. She renewed the Triple A, had the car inspected, bought emergency fluids, and headed off hoping—hoping hoping hoping—she hadn't made a bad choice.

"Well, New York, New York," the stranger said loudly. "It's a hell of a town."

"That's right," Audrey nodded.

"Funny," he said, "because I'm from New York, too."

"Really?" Sometimes it seemed everyone was your neighbor.

"From Schenectady," he nodded emphatically, smirking. "Good ol' Schenectady."

"Ah, Schenectady," said Audrey, joining him in his mockery though she knew nothing of the place. She never really had that—contempt for her hometown—but all of Molly's college friends had it. Molly probably said, "Jersey," in just the same way, like she should be entitled to claim someplace better.

"But I've been in Texas for a long time, ten years," he shrugged and took a sip of his coffee. "Since I've been married. We're down in Galveston now, by the water."

It amazed Audrey how people could end up in such faraway places—though here she was now, Audrey herself, in a faraway place. "That must be nice. Water's always nice. Are you working up here?"

He winced and made a face like a kid presented with the wrong plate of food. "Am I working?"

"Yes," laughed Audrey. "Are you working?"

"You could say that." He stretched his arms overhead and arched back over his chair. "I'm bringing a horse to my wife. You understand that there are many people on the planet, many people in Texas, who could do this with their eyes closed. For me though, it's work. It's definitely work." He held up a stapled batch of instructions, stern with boldface and bullet points

"Well," Audrey began cautiously, she didn't like getting into the subject of money. Her husband always assumed everyone secretly had it. "Isn't there a sort of trailering service you can rent?"

"Of course there is. And they've got the dough, believe me. Her parents' place, whew." He gave a long, low whistle. "This is just a test. Just a test of me."

What did that mean, Audrey wondered. In the end, her husband was often right; strangers became strange the moment you thought you might like them. That happened all the time on New Jersey Transit.

"It's just Judy, my wife," he continued. "Judy's sick—again. She's sick with something new and tragic and beyond diagnosis every day now. This time she's sure the cure is her childhood horse. So I get roped into driving up here, staying with her parents, trailering this thing, and driving it back. It took four guys to get the damn thing in the box. I just stood there. I don't know anything about horses. I'm just some guy from Schenectady, and suddenly here I am—the barnyard FedEx. That's me, the Pony Express."

He drank some coffee and then drummed on the table again. "You ever been to Schenectady?"

Audrey shook her head.

"The word means Land of the Pines. So you pine all your life and then end up here."

"What is she sick with? Your wife? May I ask?"

"She's sick of me. She's sick of living. If I got in a wreck she'd probably be the picture of health."

Audrey looked out the window and watched a paper bag ride the current across a puddle. The wind had wrapped a flag around its pole and the wet fabric hung in defeat, huddled around itself like an animal licking its wounds.

"You know," he continued. "My parents have been together for forty-four years so I've never even imagined divorce, but I think she'll do it. I think she'll divorce me."

"I'm sorry," said Audrey. There was resignation in his tone, the quiet distraction of defeat. It was familiar, but still miserable, to hear about a marriage falling apart, no matter how little you cared, how small your investment. He probably had no one to talk to.

"Well, I'm sorry I got started," he said.

"Please," said Audrey, feeling guilty at her own contentment. She was enjoying herself. It was a little like being at the movies, drinking Cokes and watching the rain. Last spring break Molly had dragged her to volunteer at the community gardens and she'd resisted that too. School groups had come; they had cleaned out the lot, dug beds, planted sweet peas, peppers, and strawberries. That, too, had been a surprising joy.

"What's the horse's name?" she asked.

"Carmen."

"Well that's nice."

"Her daddy had a Ford dealership. From a long line of car men." He rolled his eyes. "Car Men! Can you believe that? Car Men."

Audrey laughed. She liked him. He seemed fourteen, a weathered and impudent adolescent. Troubled but harmless. That was the thing about meeting new people, you were always measuring the good against the bad, assessing everything they said and did. She watched the rain beat at the window as the sky cracked with lightning, the electrified fissure straight ahead. *Give people a chance*, she used to tell Molly after her first day of school.

It was then—as Audrey thought about her daughter and what she'd say to the girl later on the phone—so suddenly it barely registered, the metal Customers Only sign she'd parked under whipped off its post, caught air like a Frisbee, and then fell—like a guillotine—through the windshield of her car. Her car? Yes, her car.

"Whoa!" said her neighbor. The glass on either side of the sign splintered and then sank, a corner of the sign poking out like a shark fin.

"That's my car," she said stunned. She slapped the table like a person witnessing brand-new technology, breakthroughs. "That's *my* car."

It was almost a relief really. There. It had happened. Disaster had struck and she'd lived to tell the tale. She giggled breathily, like someone else. "I've never seen anything like that."

"I sure wish I could buy you a beer," he said. "I sure wish we could take the edge off that one."

It was 10 AM. She'd never been offered a drink so early before. "My name is Audrey," she laughed. She held out her hand and noted the little line at her wrist. She had tan lines from her garden gloves and she was proud of them, the way her daughter used to be proud of the marks on her neck she'd get from the violin.

"Well Audrey, I'm Trent." His grip was firm and his skin smooth but not quite soft. "Hello, my name is Trent and I'm amazed."

When the rain stopped, it stopped completely. The sky broke with sun and the water began evaporating, draining, whatever it could do to so quickly disappear. A few puddles remained under cars and at the edges of the restaurant like a narrow moat.

The tow truck had come, and everyone stood and marveled at the situation, how the sign had cut through the upholstery smack in the middle of the bench front seat, how it had lodged itself deep into the stuffing and springs, how the glass stayed splintered but intact on either side.

Trent insisted on following the tow truck to the service station to make sure everything went smoothly. "I'll keep an eye out for you, lady. I'll show you some Texas."

"How's the horse?" she asked.

"In rain," he read, "provide blankets. So it's too late now, isn't it?"

"Probably." It was heating up already. The sun was high and hard at work. Audrey imagined what it might be like to live here, to go about the business of life with the sun pressing down like that. Maybe it made everyone friendlier, made strangers allies in the fight against the heat. Drive Friendly, instructed the highway signs shaped like the state.

"So, see you there," Trent said, smiling as he walked backward toward the other side of the lot.

The mechanic said hours. They could get the right windshield, but someone had to drive it over and install it. "We're talking five, six o'clock. If not tomorrow," he said, scratching his lips with greased-up fingers.

"I could just find a hotel nearby," Audrey told Trent. The rush of amazement had worn off, and now she was feeling a little sick to her stomach, like a teenager in dread of calling home, of hearing, *I told you so.*

"Well I've got an idea," offered Trent. He squinted at her as if trying to determine in advance if she'd be game. "I've got plans to look at a piece of property over in east Austin. It's just about forty miles from here, so I figured I might as well have a look while I'm in the area. But it's a beautiful drive, so if you want to come along I could bring you back here later and you won't have to spend the whole day sitting around some motel worrying."

"I'm not worrying," Audrey said quickly. "I'm not worrying at all."

Though she was. She was already slipping into a panic so intense and so common to her that her daughter often chalked it up to biology, some unfortunate symptom of menopause that rendered a person at once jittery and distracted, sorrowful and dazed. Dan would always come up with something. He could review any situation and determine exactly the point where a person, Audrey, could have, should have, known better.

"I have to go to the ladies' room." She wanted a moment alone and some water on her face.

"Well, I'll wait," said Trent, all patience and concern. "Go on."

Inside the service station she followed a cool linoleum hallway to a restroom and a pay phone with a chair beside it. Audrey sat on the edge of the vinyl seat and thought briefly of calling home, just to check in, just to say things were fine. But the conversation wouldn't go that way, she was sure. She would come unhinged under questioning. She would tell everything in one woozy rush, and Dan would end up worried and ranting. She shouldn't have to drive on with all of his skepticism prickling under her skin.

She could call Molly though. Molly would like the adventure of it all. Molly was always talking about the people she met here and there, the whole world allowed access to her orbit. She would get a kick out of Trent. She would pull her knees to her chest and give a deep, long *Really?* She would respond like it was gossip, and in a way, thought Audrey, it was. Here she was, a grown woman, a married woman, bumbling around with a married man, both of them far from home.

Maybe she should just find a hotel. She checked for a phone book, but there was just a metal cord hanging from the booth, dangling awkwardly, connected to nothing.

She called her husband. She had to. And while Audrey knew in her heart that neither the storm nor the windshield was anything to confess, she felt a tickle developing in her throat, a pinch behind her right eye, all the usual symptoms of gearing herself up for an elaborate apology. She dialed the number of her home and with each button she pressed, she felt herself moving toward an avoidable fate, like watching herself pull into a parking spot scattered with glass.

But there she went. She would end up on the phone for an hour. Dan would get on the line with the mechanic himself. She would hurry outside to Trent and end up talking fast, making excuses, letting on that all her cowboy bravado had disappeared with the rain. She would see nothing of Texas but this service station. The car would end up on a flatbed after all. Dialing two more digits could change the whole day. And in the quietest way, thinking of her own mother and the things she'd never seen, with two hands Audrey hung up the phone.

She dialed her daughter's number, punching in a calling card and waiting for the tones. She listened to four soft rings and then Molly's voice on the machine, the frank informal request for a message. Okay. All right. It was hard to decide how much to tell. "Molly, it's Mom. I'm in Texas," Audrey scanned the phone for an indication of where in Texas she might be, but there was none.

She looked around at the scuffed linoleum of the floor, the shiny linoleum on the walls, dragged her finger across a panel of it, and imagined that this must be what it was like in the bowels of a stadium, of Disneyland, of anywhere from which a person might emerge and perform. She gave a laugh she hoped would sound light, casual. "Somewhere in Texas and I am thinking of you."

Back outside Audrey was all smiles as she pulled her sunglasses from her bag. "All right," she told Trent. "Let's go." He had parked sloppily behind the service station, taking up the entire row of compact spots in the shade. The truck was a deep burgundy and the trailer was a sleek and shiny silver. "Well, isn't that something," marveled Audrey. The whole thing looked brand-new and decadent, unscuffed and glimmering in the sun like a toy. It seemed hard to believe that a creature was living back there.

"It's obscene," said Trent. "When real guys pass with their beat-up trailers I can hardly look."

"So are you sure you can actually handle this thing?" Audrey felt playful and flirtatious.

"Yeah, yeah. I may be stupid but I'm not irresponsible." Trent threw the keys in the air and caught them. Threw them again, higher, and they crashed on the pavement, spreading out in a skirt.

"Can I see the horse?" Audrey asked, picturing a deep-cinnamon-colored horse, a shiny coat, muscles rippling at its haunches. She imagined escorting it across the great stretch of Texas, pulling over to a wide sleepy field, opening the trailer door, and setting the animal free. She hadn't touched a horse since she was a girl, but she could remember the short smooth hairs of the face. She could still picture her own small hand making the long, slick stroke down the neck.

"Well, I always hate to disappoint, but I think we should wait until later. She gets so rattled when you open the door. And I just gave her water back at McDonald's and I don't want to get her riled up again. But later—on the way back." Trent looked at his watch and nodded emphatically. "That's what we'll do."

He let Audrey into the cab, and as she sat there, the fabric of the burgundy seats warm even through her jeans, she felt, for the first time, a creeping new fear that she might be making a mistake. She could hear Dan's cross-examination: *Didn't you think it was a little peculiar, a man refusing to show you his horse? Did you not think to take down a license plate, to leave the information — at least — on Molly's answering machine?*

But there was Trent, turning the key in the ignition, throwing the whole rig into gear.

"Listen," she said. "It's very kind of you to offer to entertain me, but I'm starting to think I should stay. If they do a bad job, it's my daughter who ends up with a faulty car." He should be reminded: She was somebody's mother.

"Well, that's the sad truth about these things. They could do a bad job with you standing right there, and they'd probably be right in assuming you won't know the difference. I do hate mechanics!" He laughed as he pulled onto the road.

In the passenger-side mirror, Audrey caught a glimpse of her own car waiting for care in the bright parking lot. Trent had them moving fast, up to fifty in moments, already accelerating from ramp to highway. He flicked on the radio and the truck filled with mariachi music, the tickle of guitars mixing their lines of sorrow and hope.

"You should just relax and have a nice look around. It's beautiful here," he said. "See?"

And it was beautiful—preciously beautiful—as though every sight around her was an extraordinary parting gift. The long grass around them was patched with wildflowers, small pavilions of color to break up the green. There was little but sky and field, a sprinkling of cattle, and the occasional signpost of a Texas flag, a lone star in the wind harnessed from flight. No one in the world knew where she was headed, she thought, and she might never be back. Her car might sit there unclaimed as she disappeared, by way of weather or misfortune, into some small speck of this giant state.

Or not.

She might just find herself arriving in Arizona in that punchy little Subaru only to tell Molly that, yes, she had had an adventure; yes, she had seen the land—and she'd been entirely too worried to enjoy a thing.

"You barely know me, and already you're telling me I need to relax." Audrey laughed.

Trent shrugged and kept his eyes on the road.

Granted, this trip was exceptional, but even the simplest pleasures could be impossible for Audrey to enjoy. Just last weekend there had been spring fireworks on the river and, with Dan not feeling well, she had gone alone to watch the display. Dan had even encouraged her to go. Yet, as she drove along the parked cars and the revelers lining the road, she had gotten nervous about finding a safe place to park, nervous about drunks breaking in to steal the radio, nervous about the police car behind her and whether or not the new registration had made it into the glove box or was still sitting in the kitchen by the telephone.

And so she had stayed in the car all evening, driving on through several tiny towns, past all the small parties along the road, bright with hibachis and toddlers pointing to the sky.

She caught bits and pieces of the gorgeous explosions in her rearview mirror and, on the way home, up ahead over the dash. And she resented Dan for training her to see the doom in all things, and she resented Molly for daring her to be as brave as a teen, and she resented her own preoccupation with pleasing everyone else—had she lost all faith in thinking for herself?

In the end, she told Dan and Molly that, yes, she'd sat right in the heart of things having an utterly wonderful time. And privately, she promised herself to stop letting every pleasurable experience turn into yet another instance of regret.

She imagined telling Molly and Dan proudly about this day. It was so peaceful, she would say. The truck so heavy and solid on the road. Molly would ask about Trent, if he was handsome, if he was flirtatious, if he was, well, Texas friendly. Audrey looked at him. He had the uncanny look of a boy in a man's body. His skin looked tough but he was still lean and sinewy. She could picture him still—at his age—swinging from doorways, climbing over fences, getting too drunk. His arms were covered with tiny scratches and scars.

But when Audrey looked at his face, it was certainly interesting, certainly handsome, but it was just a face—a long nose, a sharp chin, a high brow. He kept it active, amused, responsive to the world, but it was just the face of a man beside her driving on a highway to a destination she hadn't chosen but to which she'd merely consented to be taken. This was just life, life in her skin, the only way it ever felt—mildly concerned, a bit anxious, open to delight but not quite immersed in it. A step away from that always.

She pinched her lips—such a foolish-looking gesture—but something she had done since childhood when she was afraid, fear bucking about inside her on a dare as she put her head down to go. "So where is it exactly we're headed?" She asked brightly.

"Just a little ways down the road." Trent scratched at his head and let his other hand drift lazily to his lap, his two fingers suddenly the only connection to the wheel, as if making a point of being casual. "East Austin—America's favorite vacationland."

"I've heard wonderful things about Austin," Audrey offered.

"This is not the part of Austin you've been hearing about."

"Well if it's so awful, then why would we want to look at property there?" She didn't mean to sound nervous; she hoped she didn't sound nervous. "You know what they say: location, location, location."

"Well, it's bad, but it's not that bad. Or it is that bad—but it's supposed to get better. Judy's little brother, Bailey—my brother-in-law—he bought himself some awful piece of property there and he thinks I ought to do the same. But I'll tell you, when he bought his place there were holes everywhere you looked—in the floorboards, in the roof, in the walls. It was less like a house than a piece of cheese."

"He wants you to live like that?"

"No. I think he just wants to keep me in Texas even if Judy and I split. The two of us are like this," Trent took his right hand off the wheel and squeezed it into a tight fist.

"So you wouldn't go back to New York? If things don't work out?"

"No. I could never go back." He looked pensively ahead, his lips pursed as though he'd lost his train of thought. Audrey said nothing; she just watched. Why couldn't he ever go back? People were so peculiar. There was just so much history and circuitry in them, you never had any idea what was going on inside. She watched Trent scratch his cheek, his mind still lost somewhere on the horizon. She wished for something to do with her hands, so she opened her purse and began digging around in it. She felt her wallet, her tissues, her eyeglasses case.

"Anyway," Trent said suddenly, reeling himself back in from the distance. "Anyway, anyway, anyway—the house. Mind you, living in the house is just an alternate plan. A just-in-case. The real plan is something else. What Bailey wants to do, what he thinks he's going to do, is rebuild from scratch out of the Home Depot and then sell the place to Bill Gates or something. He says the neighborhood is getting better, but I don't think it's happening as fast as he thinks it is."

Audrey was always fascinated by gentrification, reverent of the people getting in at the right time. It killed her to think of the apartments they could have bought in Manhattan, but Dan had no patience to wait for a neighborhood to transform, for the risks to diminish.

"It's probably smart," she said feeling nearly envious.

"Maybe. Of course, I'd rather keep my wife than become a real estate mogul."

"Of course," she said. "I'm sorry."

"I mean, there's no place like home," he said plainly, turning to Audrey to see her response.

Did he mean no place like Galveston or like Schenectady? Or no place like beside his wife when things were romantic and new?

"There's no place like home," she repeated softly, though when she thought of home just then she thought not of the light, spare sprawl she had painstakingly decorated in northern New Jersey but instead of the small dark apartment in which she'd grown up, doilies and oilcloth on every surface, the flat broad leaves of plants gone caked in dust. She remembered climbing from step stool to countertop to reach for things to cook. Her parents had been broke and struggling, and she'd always taken care of herself. She'd told Dan stories he couldn't believe: at seven, ironing school clothes on the floor; at nine, tumbling off the fridge trying to change a high bulb. "I can't stand it," he'd say. "Stop."

She missed him suddenly very much.

Trent pulled off the highway and turned into a neighborhood lined with small, sagging houses on tiny lots cluttered with toys, bags of leaves, a rusted wheelbarrow, a porcelain sink basin streaked with rust. "We're almost there," he said.

And while Audrey had anticipated streets lined with declining houses and beat-up vehicles, she hadn't anticipated driving beyond them—to streets where the windows were either boarded up or broken, the porches collapsing, the telephone wires dangling down. At first, they passed a few people out on the street: a small child in a diaper sitting on a porch, two men in blue jeans working on a car, one of them just legs poking out from under the hood. But now, there was no one, no motion anywhere except a matted black and white dog, ambling away.

"Is this it?" she asked.

Trent nodded. "Nearly."

She reached back into her purse, remembering suddenly that she didn't even have her keys. They were back with the mechanic inside the car. Even her house keys were in her valise, tucked away inside the Subaru trunk. She had nothing at all to help her protect herself.

She laughed, an amazed burst of sound. It was absurd, it occurred to her suddenly, to think she'd be in any better shape with a sharp key held tightly in her knobby fist. She was arthritic, and there was really no where to run.

"What?" asked Trent. "Why are you laughing?"

She just shook her head and pinched her lips, trying not to think of her husband's face as she pulled out of the driveway three days ago, how he had rubbed his eyes like a tired child. He did that often in frustration and his skin showed the wear. He did few things and did them well. Investing, golf, protecting. These things. She loved him very much. She did.

Trent negotiated the tight, awkward turns until they were driving along the stone wall of a cemetery. Audrey looked at the assortment of stones, the small and tilting white ones worn nearly smooth, the grand shiny monuments declaring lives of splendor. It amazed her that no matter where you went, there were people who felt entitled to such spectacle. Audrey herself wished to be cremated, her ashes scattered, though she had never made any mention of where; she'd never decided. She liked the idea of the Brooklyn Bridge. It was one of her favorite places, yet she wasn't sure about landing all over the city—dusting the fish market and falling into the East River along with the soot of trains and buses, all that exhaust and sludge. It was the vantage point she liked, not the destination.

"Look," said Trent, "I don't think I can handle these turns with this whole back end. You don't mind walking a couple of blocks do you?"

"No," said Audrey. "That's fine." She was thinking about everything she'd seen on the trip: Pennsylvania, Virginia, Tennessee, and Arkansas, the scrub grass and deciduous trees getting darker and thicker along the way. She didn't know what was coming but, she reminded herself, she had made it through a breathtaking storm.

Trent parked next to the cemetery and they both got out of the truck.

"Well, it sure isn't a very nice neighborhood, is it now?" Trent stood tall, stretching, rolling his neck in circles.

"No," said Audrey. "It isn't."

She felt a headache coming on, the distraction of pressure behind her eyes. The air was heavy and thick, as if despite the sun and the great heat it was gearing up to rain again. Trent was saying something, but she couldn't really hear. The tall grass outside the cemetery wall was a clamor of buzzes and ticks, the arguments of birds and bugs and frogs rising from the green. There was a cluster of rose bushes overgrown to a sprawl. It was a beautiful bush, ornamented with pink blossoms all low to the ground like a Christmas tree decorated by the arm of a small child alone.

"You know," said Trent, "I would buy a house here if it meant pleasing Bailey. I love him like a brother. I do."

"Yes," she said. There had to be a way to argue with fear; there had to be a way to ignore it. Audrey squatted beside the bush and pinched one of the many buds that were tight and full, just beginning to crack with color. They were lovely. The roots were tangled with weeds, and she began pulling out tight clumps of them. It was obvious they'd encroach again within days, but she kept at it. She loved the tug of the earth, the slick rope of grass in her hands.

Trent sat down beside her and picked at the grass. "One time Judy and I were at her parents' house. We were kissing on the couch, and I said something ridiculous, something like, *I could eat you up like corn*—maybe we'd just had dinner. I was kissing her arm and we were laughing. I was so in love and so nervous, and she was so beautiful."

Trent laughed, loud and alone. Audrey stole a look at him. He was sitting cross-legged with his head thrown back, eyes closed and face to the sky. He was lovelorn and tortured and possibly crazy; he had her sitting by a cemetery and talking about corn.

"Of course," he continued, "Bailey was about fifteen and spying on us from under the stairs, and he just started cackling. He has never let me live that down. *I could eat you up like corn!*"

She could see the sweat bleeding through his blue-gray T-shirt, and it exhausted her to think of his body working so hard. But then again, it was exhausting to think of her own mind spinning itself in circles, that endless rev that kept her, always, an arm's length from the world. She tried to concentrate on the warmth on her back and on the quick, hot breeze as it fanned through her hair.

"I'd kiss her arm all the way up. We were so tremendously in love."

Audrey's knees dug into the earth as she twisted stalks around her fist and pulled so hard it felt like she was reaching deep into the soil, extracting something, like a birthing. She could distinguish the sound of every bug and bird as she worked around the small stones and the earthworms. She felt an odd and quiet joy, a feeling she'd long forgotten. For just that moment, there was no Dan, or Molly; there was just Audrey, as able and focused and peaceful as she'd been when left to her own devices as a girl.

"I'm sorry I got started," Trent said.

Don't be silly. Audrey thought she spoke, but she wasn't quite sure.

She felt a shadow come over her; it could have been Trent, or a cloud, or a plane. She wouldn't look up, and it felt like a blissful surrender.

"Come look," Trent said. She could hear him slam the truck door.

"Come on," he called to her again and, finally, she got up to join him at the trailer.

Inside, Audrey could see the horse's speckled gray head strapped in place with a harness and leash. Carmen had blue blinders on her eyes, and her nostrils were flexing wide, blowing their small white hairs around as she breathed. Audrey breathed too, a tremendous breath, as if all day she'd been unknowingly desperate for air. Her lungs felt so full it seemed she could probably float, though she knew this sensation was, more likely, not the presence of air, but the absence of fear. Or, she thought, perhaps they were the same thing. She stood beside Trent and brushed her knuckles along the horse's jaw. Carmen was old and overweight, but Audrey could imagine her at a grassy riverbed, gracefully stopping to drink. She imagined the coat beading with sweat, simultaneously dried and inspired by the weighty sun. "There, there," Audrey said, brushing aside tufts of coarse, white mane, like they were the bangs of a feverish child. She drew a palm along the horse's back where the hair was short and smooth, the skin warm and pulsing. Was it so ludicrous to admit that she wanted to ride?

"She is impossibly beautiful," Audrey said.

And maybe she kissed Trent because she was grateful and relieved, and it was too hot to think straight, or because half the country had already passed under her wheels, or because her daughter was waiting in Arizona, doubting that Audrey would have anything to tell. Or maybe she did it because of the graveyard beside her, its bright white stones weathered flat to chalk. Whatever the case, she pushed up on her toes, her loafers pressing into the give of the earth, and she rose to his lips to kiss him.

She rubbed a thumb along his eyebrow, smoothing it toward the outside of his face. He looked surprised, grateful, and curious. It was very still, and except for that moment of connection and pressure, she felt small and teary and impermanent.

They parted at Pep Boys, where her car was waiting, finished, in the parking lot. There were well-wishes, a handshake, an exchange of nervous gratitude. She drove off through the hill country of central Texas, through the red shifting tables of New Mexico, through the thick desert scrub growing out of the Arizona sand. She drew her right hand along the fissure of the front seat, the crack revealing the foam, the plastic and springs. She held her hand there as she drove, as if to remind herself that everything really had happened—she'd dared a tornado, weeded faraway ground, kissed some kind of cowboy, and continued west, racing against the turn of the earth as it kept on moving.

Such
a Big
Mr. England

It's almost too much for Alfred to handle in one weekend—the death of Princess Diana and a visit from his first grandchild—but he's doing the best he can. At breakfast this morning he took pictures of the baby as she spittled and cooed before ducking into the bedroom to catch the latest on CNBC.

At the beach for lunch, he held Allegra on his lap in the low sand chair and marveled—the tininess of her feet! the small perfection of her toes!—before pleading hay fever and heading home to get back on the phone.

It isn't his fault that he can't concentrate on the baby. Not exactly it isn't. Not really. For one thing, she's an ugly baby, ugly beyond the strawberry mark in a ring around her eye, spotting her like a cartoon dog. But it isn't just that.

Since Diana's death yesterday, Alfred's phone has been ringing nonstop. He has been busy taking sympathy calls and fielding questions from friends, from acquaintances, from relatives in retirement communities all over the country: *Where will she be buried? Will Charles remarry? Will the queen ever hand down the crown?*

It's true, Alfred knows some things about the princess.

He knows that Diana, on her father's side, is related to Winston Churchill.

He knows just how much Ronald Reagan spent on a wedding gift for Charles and Di—seventy-five grand for a cut-glass vase.

He knows that for Diana's father the wedding had been no easy feat. Since his first stroke, Earl Spencer Sr. had never managed to walk so steadily as he did escorting Di down the aisle at St. Paul's Cathedral.

About himself, Alfred just knows that he is finding a far greater satisfaction in having become an authority on the royal family than he is in having become a grandpa, in holding his son's new baby.

All day he has felt that his attention has not been where it should be. But each time he vows to keep his head in the moment, his kind heart and warm lap extended toward this small, new family member, he finds himself thinking about the princess, her little princes, her funeral plans, and the rising tide of flowers outside Kensington Palace.

But now, in the light of the late afternoon, as his family prepares the last barbecue of the summer, Alfred has brought the portable phone out to the patio and is finishing up his last call, he swears.

"I'm so sorry," says his cousin Adele from Phoenix, offering simply her condolences as though Diana were *Alfred's* princess, as though her death were something that had happened to him.

"Thank you," says Alfred. "Thank you very much."

"Would you believe this?" his wife, Miriam, laughs, hearing Alfred on the phone. "We've got Mr. England over here."

"Who knew you were marrying so well?" quips their son,

Benjamin, calling out through the kitchen window as he rinses farm-stand zucchini and tomatoes for the shish kebabs.

"How on earth did *that* happen?" Ben's wife, Elise, raises an eyebrow and purrs to the baby, who is beside her, belly-up in the portable playpen. "How did Grandpa Alfred get to be such a big Mr. England?"

It began with an eggcup—a bone-china throne for a soft-boiled egg. It was hand-painted on the side, a portrait of Charles and Di framed lavishly in banners of gold. Alfred saw it displayed in a midtown window on a red velvet stand surrounded by jewel-encrusted eggs. It was 1981, shortly before the July wedding, the middle of what had already proven to be a good year. Alfred was, at the time, fifty-two years old. He had brought in a lot of money that year and still had never bought himself an object of value. He'd bought a piano for Miriam and fancy schooling for Benjamin, but he'd never before had a collectible, a decorative object, something without a real use. He stared, fascinated.

He liked the shape of the piece—like a figure eight with either end lopped off, like a miniature hourglass. He liked the feel of the smooth thin china against his open palm. Mostly, though, he was tickled by the great pomp of it, the idea of twenty-two-carat leafing in honor of the royals, in honor of an egg, in honor of himself, Alfred—and that he had become a person who could actually have such a thing in his home. He stood outside the window for a long while before striding into the store. "How much for the eggcup in the window," he sang, giddy with something, his stomach racing and alive. It had been the start of something.

Visiting guests and relatives would gravitate to the curio shelves built into the foyer wall, which were finally, after twenty years in the house, beginning to fill. What had once just housed the fire extinguisher and emergency flashlight now contained a battery of royal wares, including a china vase with the Spencer family crest and a tin of mints embossed with the profile of Prince Charles. There was a Buckingham Palace commemorative plate, a Queen Elizabeth dinner bell, a videotape of Charles and Di's wedding that had come with collector's playing cards. And the tea towels! All the tea towels! Alfred had even been given one printed with a photo of himself. "Unbelievable!" he'd marveled. "I'm the world's first Jew on a tea towel!"

Suddenly, after a lifetime of receiving gift certificates he'd just pass off to his wife, Alfred began getting presents, real presents in boxes wrapped with paper and bows. Alfred finally had a hobby, an identity, an expertise.

The night of Diana's death, after taking the first flurry of late-late phone calls, Miriam sat beside Alfred in front of the TV. She teased in a singsong: "I think someone's enjoying this . . ."

"It's not that I don't think it's a tragedy," Alfred sheepishly responded. "I do think it's a tragedy. I really do."

While he is certainly not happy about what has happened to Diana, for the first time in his life everyone he knows wants his opinion and, further, is interested in how he feels. He's entitled to this, really, he reasons, this fifteen minutes of fame.

So leave it to his son's family to arrive this morning, visiting for a week from California, demanding his attention, and mocking him in his own home.

From Elise: "Who's upset about Diana? Every divorcée in the modern world and my father-in-law. Just stricken."

From Benjamin: "We spent almost a year brewing you up your own personal princess. C'mon, Dad, we came all this way."

From Miriam: "Your first grandchild! Your legacy."

His legacy? Alfred can't even look—this kid is a horror. Her nose, for example, isn't the simple, doughy slope of a normal baby but hooked (already!); and rather than the usual lipless baby smile, Alfred's granddaughter's lips are red and full, stretching across her whole face when she smiles, lifting to expose the sharp line of her gums. He finds the need to keep turning away from her—to the wall, to the phone, to the TV screen—as though to clear his visual palate before taking another look. But then he looks back and there she is—still ugly, the poor kid. The ugly Allegra. It kills him.

"All of Elise's good, blue-blood, Goyisha genes," he'd said to Miriam earlier, "and we end up with a kid who looks just like us."

Miriam shushed Alfred and swatted at his face. It was a terrible thing to say, he knew, but it was true; he'd been hoping for better. Didn't Miriam remember the rows of blondes on the bride's side at the wedding? Didn't she remember that among them there had been Astors and Duponts?

———

Now, outside at the patio table, Alfred pushes the button to hang up the portable phone and it emits a high, pained chirp as the line disconnects.

Beside him, Benjamin is cutting up the vegetables, raising the moist smell of fresh earth with every slice. He deftly slides the pieces onto metal skewers, which he sets in a neat row on a clean, glass plate. Ben's wife, Elise, is husking corn into a brown paper bag and has not broached the subject of composting—not yet. Alfred watches stray corn silk disappear into her hair, which is so light, it seems, it won't ever show gray. Miriam is in the kitchen preparing Cornish game hens in marinade, Alfred's newfound favorite dish. "They stay so much moister than big chickens," he explains to Elise. "I was almost ready to leave poultry to the birds."

"It's just fat. They've just got a greater surface area of fat from the skin," Elise says plainly, knowing better.

When his earlier efforts at the supermarket had been dismissed, Alfred decided to whip up his own dish. He snuck off to Say Chih's at the Potunk Road mini mall and got all the types of dumplings—shrimp, chicken, and veggie. Now he smacks his lips, rubbing his hands together over his offering, "Ah, dumplings. Ah, little dumplings. These are meatless," he tells Elise, who shakes her head to decline.

Instead she nods toward the playpen, trying to urge Alfred there, "Speaking of dumplings . . ." she trails off, looking at the baby.

"Yes. Speaking of dumplings," Alfred says dutifully. He walks to the playpen and bends down to hoist up the baby, Allegra, who is, at ten months, already sturdy and dense. "We sure packed a lot of baby into that baby!" is what Ben likes to say. At birth Allegra weighed in at well over ten pounds.

In his effort to role-play the good grandpa, Alfred holds the baby stiffly against his chest for a moment and then stretches both his arms above him, lifting Allegra high in the air. His baby! His baby's baby! His doll of dolls—Allegra!

"Easy there, now, Dad," says Ben as Alfred sets the baby back down.

With Allegra back in her pen, Alfred looks hopefully to the phone set down on the table, to the vee of birds overhead, to pretty Elise with her lap full of corn, and then back to the baby, the still-ugly baby. He steps away, closer to the house.

"Allegra, Allegra, Allegra," he says. "You just can't shorten it. We picked Benjamin so he could go by Benji and Ben, BJ. We even used to call him Shoes."

Elise puts down her corn and smiles at Alfred, with her smug combination of mockery and good cheer. "There's no reason I can see that you still can't call her Shoes."

"Do you know that about Benji?" asks Alfred proudly. "That all the kids at school and at soccer—for years—everyone used to call him Shoes?"

"No," Elise says.

"I told you that," laughs Ben, "I did."

And here it is again, thinks Alfred, that nothing he offers holds weight with this woman. Does he have nothing to contribute at all? He and Miriam offered to fly out after the baby was born and what did Elise say? "No. No. You shouldn't. We want nuclear family time."

Which is why it's hard for Alfred to understand Elise as "laid back," the way Benji describes her. Sometimes she strikes Alfred as too brisk and no nonsense, always presenting Miriam with house gifts of expensive kitchenware in sleek black boxes—the Swedish Water Filterer, the Belgian Waffler, the German Mincer. What does she have in mind!

"Work!" he exclaims, "How's work? Do you still work much together?" Both Ben and Elise earn the same salary at the same environmental consulting firm.

"We'll get to go on-site together sometimes," Ben says, glowing. "Not always but every so often."

Alfred believes these jobs, these terms like "going on-site," are just fancy names for driving around California together. When Elise and Ben were in college, they'd spend spring breaks driving around the country's deserts and parks, and now, Alfred is sure, they have miraculously found a way to do so for money. He pictures their lives as just one big northern California road trip, only in addition to filling up at gas stations, Ben and Elise have to take a small sample of the ground. Alfred imagines Ben digging up a small anthill in the blacktop, adding fluid to it from a dropper and reading toxin levels by simply noting any color change. He imagines Elise jotting down findings on a clipboard while Ben steps into the food mart for mini donuts before they get back on the road.

Elise excuses herself, pads barefoot across the brick patio, up the steps, and into the house. Benjamin pushes the plate of kebabs safely to the center of the table and bends over the playpen, heartily lifting Allegra up to his chest. He sits again, bouncing the baby on his lap, holding her hands in his and directing them toward the appropriate body parts as he chants: "Miosis! Mitosis! My-knee-sis and my-nose-sis!"

The sun rests warmly on Alfred's arms for a moment before sinking just behind the neighbors' tree. He watches his son, feeling both proud and embarrassed of Ben's big love for this baby—the booby baby, the lackluster prize. Alfred sits in a patio chair right across from Ben, watching Allegra bounce. Her cheeks vibrate, her eyes shake, her tongue lolls. Her right eye seems planted farther in her skull than her left—the optical illusion of the red ring around the socket. Alfred detects the right eye wandering off to the side, looking lazily and lost toward the west. Is that an illusion too, or is it the genetic reprise of Benji's own lazy eye he had finally learned to control as a teen? Could he, Alfred, be responsible for this doomed inheritance?

Alfred takes a deep, sudden breath—a bitter gulp of air. Is he nauseated at the sight of his own grandchild? Ashamed, he shuffles his chair closer and touches Allegra's soft, bulbous heels, notes the deep shadow lines that separate her toes.

"Miosis!" Benjamin sings, "Mitosis! My arm and my-elbow-sis!"

"Everything," Alfred tries to interject with wonder, "biology even, just a song for this baby."

"Little birds!" exclaims Miriam, stepping out of the house,

light-footed yet careful on the wooden steps. "These are the best. Our new fave."

On a white ceramic serving dish are four local game hens, tiny and shaking under their yellow, uncooked skins. In an effort to make a mealtime peace, Alfred winks at Elise, an insider's conspiracy, and Elise winks back expertly, even smiling in return.

Miriam sets the plate down and looks at the grill—a closed-up and smokeless three-legged pod. "Oh. Nobody started the grill," she notes and heads toward the side of the house where they keep the charcoal.

"I've got it," Alfred stops her, embarrassed. He just can't seem to get himself on the ball. "Just a minute."

He hefts a nearly full bag of coal up on his hip and lets the briquettes tumble into the well of the grill. He squeezes the plastic container of lighter fluid twice, so that it squirts and wheezes, and squirts again. He drops in a match and the flames rise orange and thin, and the smoke pulls up in a curl, eastward over the head of the baby and into the sky that is still quietly light. He likes feeling useful, has always earned his keep. He's not good at being retired like Miriam is.

In the last year Miriam has planted a garden, joined a book group, and signed up for several weekend courses at the community center. She is always asking Alfred if he wants to sign up with her—a class in watercolors, car maintenance, conversational French. Alfred always says no, by which he doesn't necessarily mean he doesn't want to. He's never been good at describing his wants. He just means that he can think of too many reasons not to sign up, of other things he should be doing. "Like what?" Miriam asks. "Like what?"

Mostly, he paces the house and reads the papers while Miriam is out painting or welding or updating her Web site. She took a one-week class and put up a Web site. It's just her name, her picture, and a list of a few of the things she likes—not far from a centerfold bio, she jokes—but Miriam has a Web site for god's sake, and 167 people have visited it so far. In the class, they taught her to install a counter.

Miriam lifts Allegra out of the playpen, off the soft flannel sheets and away from the smoke. She cradles the baby in one arm and touches lightly at the face, dabbing her fingertips gently at the bright spot encircling Allegra's eye.

Miriam has read that such blood-filled marks can be treated with laser therapy. "They say it's a five- to ten-minute procedure," she says to Elise, nodding in an effort to be both encouraging and casual. "Then if the skin doesn't shrink properly, it can be corrected with cosmetic surgery."

Elise gets up to take the baby away. "The doctor says most strawberry marks fade by the time a child is nine." says Elise. She believes in breast-feeding and midwifery and kept the placenta for over a month Saran-Wrapped in the freezer.

"Nine years is a long time," Alfred says.

"Well, we're discussing it," Elise pulls the baby in close to her chest.

Who knows what nine years will bring! Who knows whether Alfred will even be alive for the day that growth, life, and sun will have stretched and faded the mark away. "Give that kid a break," he mumbles.

"Hey Benji," says Elise dismissively, "maybe we should go for a quick run before dinner. We don't eat like this at home," she turns to Miriam, "from one big meal to another."

There. Another refusal.

"Hens cook quickly," Ben explains. "I don't think we have time. Do we, Mom?"

Miriam shakes her head no. Elise, like a spoiled child, kicks her sneakers at an anthill in the bricks.

Running running, thinks Alfred. Play play. Doesn't anyone actually have to deal with the tension they create for themselves? Or, Alfred wonders, is this a privilege reserved solely for himself? He dips a shrimp dumpling into the plastic container of soy sauce and watches the oil swirl around like a flouncing rainbow skirt. He heads for the living room to sit on the couch in front of the TV.

The mute pictures on screen are of the princess's black Mercedes crumpled under the tunnel alongside the Seine, but Alfred can only see half the screen at a time. The handle of the jog stroller is blocking the picture, breaking it up into two segments. If Alfred sits tall in his seat he can see the French civilians leaning over the retaining wall and craning their necks. If he slumps he can see below the silhouetted handle into the tunnel itself, the camera lingering on the wreckage inside. It is footage Alfred has seen a dozen times already. Yet, as he bobs up and down, up and down on his couch, he can't rise above his resentment for this obstructed view.

Upon arriving this morning, Ben immediately set himself and his tools down on the living room floor between the couch and the TV.

"What *is* that?" Alfred had asked.

"It's a jog stroller," Ben explained, not even looking up. "This way Elise and I can keep running together without either of us having to stay home with the baby."

Alfred looked at the stroller. He had seen such contraptions being pushed down the side of the road, but he had never had this close a look before. It reminded him of many things at once. It had three wheels, like a tricycle, but the front wheel jutted out a few feet ahead in order to keep the center of balance low. It had a cloth-slung chair for the baby, like a regular stroller would, but it was made of the same bright, neon fabrics as the kites he saw flown over the beach. It had one long handle that shot out the back for Elise or Ben to hold on to, to guide the stroller along as they ran behind it. There was a leash attached to the handle as a safety measure, and on back of the baby's seat, there was the same type of reflective triangle that marked an Amish buggy. It seemed a terribly elaborate chariot for an infant to ride in, the gross product of years of technology assembled into a Yuppie baby's throne.

"It was wonderful," Elise had reflected earlier as she sat down on the couch. "I came home from the hospital with the baby and this was waiting in the foyer with a bow."

"That's very nice," Alfred had offered halfheartedly.

Alfred had watched Ben inflate each of the three tires and attach them to the frame.

"Shall we go?" Ben asked Elise right after breakfast. "Hey, Dad, will you get the door?"

Alfred had held the screen open as Ben hoisted the stroller out onto the lawn. He watched as they strapped the baby into the seat and then sat down on the grass to stretch and lunge. As Ben and Elise took off in easy strides down the road, Alfred's back clenched. It was his own granddaughter in that chariot, he knew, but he had felt something so strange.

Now, from his seat in the living room, Alfred can hear the shrill ring of the portable phone break through the thin chatter outside.

"I'll get it," Elise rolls the words throatily, the drumroll preceding a good deed. "Hello?"

Alfred closes his eyes and counts, to five, six, seven, before Elise continues.

"He can't come to the phone right now. He's gearing up for some quality time with his new granddaughter, but maybe I can help you." Elise's giggles are high and light, the chirps of a naughty sorority girl.

"That's a very English move," she continues. "I mean, eventually the queen will have to say *something*."

Alfred feels something odd in his stomach, the humbled affront of someone cutting him in line.

"Yeah well, my whole family's English," says Elise. Then: "I will. I will send him your sympathies." She hangs up the phone.

Inside the house, Alfred says quietly, "You can't have that. You can't have that, too."

He watches the TV flash from photos of Diana to the local weather map. The radar shows the quick progress of storms that will move in and then disappear in the rush of new weather to come. He feels socked in the stomach, like all the wind in the world has passed through him and gone.

"You know how I really feel about the English?" he says loudly, getting up from the couch and heading back outside. "When Miriam and I went to England, I asked a waiter at breakfast how the melon was, and do you know what he said? Do you know how he answered? He said, 'I don't know sir, I haven't stuck my finger in it.' That's what he said. Fuck the English," Alfred proclaims as he slides open the screen door.

"Pardon his French," Benjamin murmurs to Elise and then, blushing, looks down at his shoes. Shoes' shoes, Alfred sadly notes, I've embarrassed him.

Miriam holds a glazing brush in one hand, upward, as though it is Lady Liberty's raised torch instead of a mere cooking tool wet with marinade—dripping soy and vinegar, oil and garlic, down the side of her hand. She looks around quickly, like an animal aware that something is wrong and unsure what move to make. She rests the brush on the edge of the dumpling plate, the sauce-covered bristles spreading out in a fan. "I'm sorry you lost your princess," she looks up to Alfred as she speaks, softly and unsure. He hates to think that he is, right at this moment, breaking her heart. He hates to imagine all the ways he's ever let her down.

"I want to tell a story," Alfred says. "I want to tell you a story, Elise."

Alfred steps out onto the landing. Miriam has already arranged the little birds, belly-down, over the sweet spot on the grill.

Before he began his collection of royalty memorabilia, Alfred had owned only one object of value, and he had owned it, himself, just for a day. It was a planter—a great, ornate, ceramic bowl that rested on a curved iron stand. It had been given to Alfred's mother on the occasion of his birth, his father presenting it with a great sweep of the arm. The stock market crashed just four days later, and then the Great Depression began, but the planter was kept. It was never filled with soil and planted for fear of damage and decrease in its resale value, but it was kept, untouched, in a corner through the years.

The only thing that had ever been placed inside the planter was Alfred himself, as an infant in a blanket the day it had been brought home. There had been a picture taken of this moment, though Alfred couldn't determine if he'd ever seen it or only heard it described. He had looked several times through all of his mother's papers, and he'd never found the picture. But, if he closes his eyes, he can still imagine being in the bowl, surrounded by the porcelain paint before it had spun its web of textureless cracks. He can vaguely recall the echo off the walls of the bowl, the whoosh of the slick hollow like a seashell's sound, a sense of height in his belly from the tall, thin, legs of the stand.

Alfred wants to say something about this to Elise—some of it, all of it, about small efforts to reclaim it, maybe—but he isn't sure what. Instead, he just sits on the wooden landing, stretching his legs out until the last step hits the back of his ankles and his toes point straight up, like the feet of a man in a grave.

The birds on the grill are still yellowy beige, though the fat under the skin has suddenly begun to whistle and spit like a grandstand, the grill alive with the crowd sounds of baseball fans. The baby is splayed out diagonally across the square of the pen, wide awake, lying on her back and quietly sucking her fingers. Her eyes are open—darting and bright. Alfred looks around the crib, noting what it is the baby might see: the shading green of the maple, the brick of the patio, the soft blue of the sky, the whole world just sweeps and planes of light and dark and colors.

As he is about to speak, to tell Elise to keep her hands off his phone and his fame, Elise picks up Allegra and sets her on Alfred's lap. The baby rests warmly against him, gives a contented gurgle, and blinks her eyes slowly and gracefully once. The strawberry mark is softer in the dusky light, and her eyes are wide, eager, looking only at Alfred. Instead of feeling the same odd repulsion, a sensation occurs in Alfred and he can only think to call it bliss. In it is the sizzle of the hens, the sky steadily absorbing more blue, and the warmth and weight of Allegra turning in his lap as she tries to reach for his collar, his ears, his face. With all this new life bustling in his lap he thinks, this must be it. His breath is short; he can hardly breathe. He lifts the baby and tries to hand her back to Elise, but she is insulted, it seems, frustrated and appalled.

"What do you want from me?" Elise asks him, beseechingly. "Why won't you like this baby? I'm just sorry you don't like my baby."

With one hand she pulls her long, light hair from her face, and with the other she gestures to Alfred with her palm up. "What do you want from me?" she asks him again, as though she is about to offer it—anything—to him on a plate.

Alfred is struck dumb by this question. He can vaguely hear his own mother asking him the very same one but lacking any urgency, any offering forward of the naked palm. His mother's words were strictly rhetorical, a frustrated, "What do you want from me, what have I got to give?"

But there is Elise, still above him. "What do you want," she says, her voice becoming urgent and genuine, the voice of a mother trying to make a child eat.

He looks around for a moment—to Ben at the table, Miriam at the grill, and the sunflowers along the neighbor's fence, slouching under their own weight—and what he sees seems plenty, certainly enough. "I would like to take the birds off the hot spot on the grill so they'll take a little longer to cook," he begins, the words coming to him, from somewhere, seeming to just slip up his throat as though it doesn't matter what he says, just that he's been so cordially invited to speak. "I don't care if they dry out or anything. I'd like enough time to get the baby set up in the jog stroller and take her for a nice walk, just down the block, maybe to the bay. Then, I'd like to come back for dinner."

"We can do that," Elise says, and Ben is already up and going for the stroller. Elise lifts the baby into the harness and belts her in before tugging socks onto her small, thick feet. The air is about to go deep blue and is already damp, skidding with mosquitoes.

"You're all set, Pop," Elise slips the leash loop over Alfred's hand. He wraps the slack several times around his wrist and then grabs on to the stroller handle. He walks over the grass and down the drive with measure, he imagines, like Earl Spencer Sr., moving proudly to give his Diana away to something grander, something huge. Alfred pushes the stroller in an even, steady gait onto the street, which seems as long and straight to him as the great aisle walk of St. Paul's Cathedral.

Here
Beneath
Low-Flying
Planes

Janie has always been blonde—or not always, but long enough to get used to it. In high school, she sprayed Sun-In from the pump and alternated blow-dryers as they overheated and cooled down, overheated and cooled down, her long brown hair streaking a buttery yellow.

In college, she switched to a stiff mix of peroxide and powdered bleach, stripping the pigment and toning to platinum with Miss Clairol White Lady from the professional beauty supply store.

During the course of her pregnancy, she has given up her age-old habits of Diet Coke and Marlboros—of course—but also hair dye, wary of the bleach saturating the scalp, making way to the blood, to the baby. She is otherwise very shower-and-go, but all this blonde over all these years has amounted to a sleek wardrobe and a collection of pin-up girl nicknames that don't quite fit with this dull brown shag, this sloppy hood of a bob, her dark eyes deep and fleckless in the bathroom mirror. It's just hair—but it's a problem.

Right now, for example, she cannot concentrate on the way Otis (happy, healthy, and fat) is suckling her left breast, or the fact that she is holding him awkwardly with just one arm. The other, stubbornly still in its hospital wristband, is drifting up carelessly to finger her hair.

Come on, Janie! Keep your hands on that baby.

"I know it's late," she tells her best friend Hazel on the phone, and it is late—past midnight now. "But listen. Forget the baby gifts, just come here, pretty please, and fix this hair."

Since college, Hazel has donned plastic gloves to measure out bleaches and toners, applying the mixture from bowl to brush to root, keeping Janie Janie. Eighty thousand dollars of education and this is still what she's best at: playing with hair, dyeing and cutting. She works for the movies. She's union.

"Say when," says Hazel, who is stretched across her queen-size bed, naked but awake, her yellow sheet twisting off in a curl, an umbilical cord to the floor. In some strident assertion of single-hood, Hazel owns her East Village one-bedroom, the bathtub in the kitchen, the bar scene buzzing below.

"Now would be terrific," laughs Janie. "Or tomorrow would be good. I'm a little hung up on my hairdo. I'd hate like hell to drop the baby."

"Have bleach; will travel," says Hazel. "I can't wait to see you. You and Jeff and Otis. Your whole little family."

Otis is a week old, but Janie is just days home from the hospital. She has wanted no guests—until now. Now she really wants guests, a small circus to step between her and her life, to perform tricks and spark spectacles, to visit and then go.

"And bring T.J.," says Janie. "Is T.J. with you?"

T.J. is Janie's little brother, and he is, in fact, splayed out beside Hazel. He is resting his chin on her knee and rolling his blue hooded eyes up at her with great concern. He hasn't seen the baby yet, but he knows that labor was traumatic and that Janie has been tired and grim.

"He's here. He's naked. We're naked," says Hazel, a little giddy with permission. She is nothing of an exhibitionist but has come—finally—to accept that Janie is not at all mad about this recent coupling of best friend and baby brother, despite the age gap of six years.

Mad? Are you kidding? Janie loves this affair, T.J.'s lifelong crush come true. Besides, now Janie can summon her world with just one call. How easy it is to assemble her troops! T.J. and Hazel are the only living people Janie would never rebuke (her mother died when she was a girl). They are a team now, and they are on her side.

"I'll let you go," Janie says. She gives quick, precise directions. "So tomorrow. See you tomorrow."

Through some miracle of foresight, planning, and Manhattan's skyrocketing real estate, Janie and Jeff have managed to sublet their deluxe apartment while they rent a three-bedroom house in Montauk for the year at an off-season rate, a fifth of the monthly sublet money going right into a mutual fund. This way, they can both take the baby's whole first year off work. There are pine barrens and deer, beaches and feathery dunes. They have a sunroom and a perfect patch of yard. If there's time, Jeff might take a science class at Southampton College, something in Environmental Studies. Janie might take painting. They can buy organic produce in East Hampton, fresh seafood down the road. In the spring, they'd like to plant a garden—their own short-term family commune.

They can even return to their jobs after this hiatus—he to an industrial architecture firm, she to PR for educational TV. *All you have to do is ask,* marvels Jeff. *Or at least work for a small, liberal firm and ask.*

A brilliant idea this seemed—but now Janie would give just about anything to be back in her own home, if not her own body. While she never had particularly romantic notions of childbirth—never, for example, wanted it on video—she couldn't have predicted such a botch job as this. Let us say only that there was too much medication given far too late, wracking her body with fruitless contractions. When she slipped into shock and her blood stopped clotting, there could be no epidural, the shot in the spine to upstage the pain. Pain! Like organs shredding, like eardrums exploding, like a charge to the gut with a redwood tree. Then, despite the clotting concern, they went ahead with the episiotomy, making the cut from vagina to rectum, that no man's land become Otis's doorway.

Nursing hurts, sitting hurts. Three days ago she milked herself with a pump. "I am woman," she said. "I am dairy queen." And now here she is—marooned—nothing around but sand and sea, no one to talk to but Jeffrey.

Jeffrey, who has taken to parenthood without any irony, without any trace of regret.

Jeffrey, who keeps asking for a recap of labor, something akin to a highlight reel.

Jeffrey, who in the delivery room, in the recovery room, and now, still, insists on rubbing Janie's back in long, slow circles—more hands on her body—and he whispers all night: *I love you, Suzy Q.*

He is driving her crazy.

T.J. and Hazel set the alarm for seven with nothing but good intentions. The clothes are put on, but the clothes come off. There is Hazel, her long black hair tumbling to the floor as she bends over to brush it, her T-shirt lifting to reveal her skinny back, the tag of her underpants poking up from her jeans.

A quick tuck, a quick kiss along the stretch of her spine. T.J. can't help it. He's been waiting since college—since *she* was in college—and he would visit the girls, crash on their floor. How he would follow Hazel around, sitting in on those classes: *Women in Film; Costuming in the Depression; Women in Costumes in the Depression.* Okay! Anything at all. *So what do you think,* she'd ask later at a party while whatever belligerent boyfriend she had was off refilling their beers.

And he would answer every question, meet every challenge, like he was driving into the black of night without headlights, just faith, determined to not take his foot off the gas for a moment. His fear has always been that Hazel will attribute any hesitation to a lack of confidence, to immaturity. But as long as T.J. keeps on with assurance, he is sure that he can win her for good. After all, no one believed him, but he has always known they would be together. He signed away his heart to her years ago.

And now this. Finally this. Clothes are put on and come right off again.

Still, it is just nine o'clock as they head over the Triborough bridge, T.J.'s Honda filled with music and bagels from Zabar's. The skyline to the right is crisp in winter sun, gleaming like a key or a serrated blade. It is just noon as they pass the wind-milled towns of the Hamptons on the last stretch to Montauk, the very tip of Long Island. A white paper bag skids down the road ahead and heaves itself up, catching air—triumphant. T.J. laughs, because everything here is triumphant; this thin strip of road is surrounded by beach. There is a pocket of pine preserve and then only sand and dune, water and sky, the colors so simple and crisp they look pasted on. The house is easy to find, small and quaint, the shingling weathered to a soft gray, the shutters painted a clean fresh white, a crib and a bench swing on the front porch.

"Finally," says Janie, swinging the door open wide. "What took you so long?" She has Otis in arm and he is wide awake.

"Your baby!"

"Look at your baby!"

Otis is wrapped in a heathery green blanket, the giant treat of him like an overstuffed spinach tortilla. There are kisses and hugs, oohs and ahs. Everyone comments on his shock of black hair: *How very punk rock! How very troll!* Then they all settle at the kitchen table, passing Otis around like he is a joint.

Wherever she lives, Janie always has a good kitchen, sunny and comfortable, a perfect place to laze around. In this house, there is a greenhouse add-on, a toasty little breakfast nook with bench seating against the glass and a scatter of chairs around the rest of the table. Janie cracks a window, propping it open with a baby book. "That's all right, right?" she asks. "Not too much for the baby?"

Everyone looks at each other and nods, coming to a wordless consensus, though nobody really knows. *Do you know? I don't know.* It is the group's first baby, and everyone's a little nervous, but it is okay. The room is hot and bright with glare and the breeze feels good on everyone. Jeff bounces the baby in his lap. Janie lies on her side on the red corduroy cushion of the banquette. She likes the feel of her back against the cold window glass.

"So," says T.J. "Tell us the cute things. How is it going, being a sassy new mom?"

"You're such a girl, T.J. You're more of girl than I am," says Janie. "You always want all the wee moments, all the schmaltz and good vibes."

T.J. laughs, his chest heaving, turning sound into smile. Hazel loves that he is completely unafraid to laugh at himself. Similarly, he is unafraid of declaring love, of making others around him feel happy and secure. Hazel has never known such confidence—which brings us to a few points about Hazel. It is her story too; it is everyone's story.

One thing is that Hazel strikes quite a figure. She is five foot ten without her boots on and her hair is long and shiny. She has a tattoo of small flowers braceleting her right wrist, the most hopeful little blossoms rendered knowingly in black.

She is spirited but wary, social but self-sufficient. She is not much of a believer in romance. Her own parents were at one time joyful—she's seen the old photos of them tan and toasting on the Cape. But in her youth they took to arguing, over anything, over nothing, canceling years of plans and parties and settling silently in front of separate TVs. Still, they do this, and Hazel is ever cautious of the shift from compromise to sacrifice, from comfort to contempt.

She has long vowed never to marry, and so she is a habitual dater of strapping, not-so-young cameramen and grips. Men given to flighty behavior and motorcycles. Men who are fairly well into their thirties and still running around work in ZZ Top T-shirts, overgrown teenagers grown thickish around the middle. And now—ha ha!—she is actually dating a teenager. Or not actually, but close.

Could she be such a hag? T.J. is just twenty-two for god's sake, but with him all of her skepticism has gone soft. Lately, she has found herself grinning and optimistic, giddy and daydreaming about the future. She has found herself growing attached. How will she ever manage to escape this one? Her best friend's brother! She'll know him for the rest of her life.

Which is why right now, as Janie teases T.J. about what a sappy uncle he'll be, Hazel looks at his unlined and hopeful face, and she imagines sneaking away. She could, without explanation, catch a train back to the city and call up some beefy ex. She could get out of this mess before it's too late.

But there is T.J.'s hand reaching for hers under the table. She thinks of the train, the city, and the beach down the street.

"I swear, T.J., if it were your baby," says Janie. "We'd be sitting through home movies right now, this early, eight days in." Janie turns her face into the corduroy cushion. She often laughs like that, quietly and hiding her face.

It is almost heartbreaking for Jeff to see Janie this happy. He has been trying so hard all week and he is a little jealous right now, jealous and embarrassed, that he hasn't been what she needed—he hasn't been fun. "So maybe we should celebrate," he says. "Maybe we should crack some beers."

"Yeah," says T.J.

"Okay."

"What the hell," says Janie. "It's past noon."

Jeff carries Otis to the fridge and grabs some microbrewery beers. Hazel switches on the transistor radio by the sink and "Love Love Me Do" fills up the room.

T.J. uses his T-shirt to twist off everyone's bottle caps, and finally Janie sits up. She's up and she is lifting her bottle.

"To Otis," she says, winking at him.

"To Janie," says Jeff.

"To Janie and Otis," says T.J.

"Yes," says Hazel. And over the baby books and paper plates, the mess of sesame seeds and crumbs, the four cross bottle necks and drink.

This, Janie thinks, is exactly what she needed, some distraction and spirit. "All right already. We've talked baby and toasted. Now, for the hair. Can we get to the hair?"

"Let's go," says Hazel. She unpacks her bag and arranges everything on the counter: a brown bottle of peroxide, a white one of bleach, bowls and brushes, and rubber gloves. There are hair clips, cotton balls, a tub of Vaseline, and a big sheet that she casts out before her, everyone transfixed for a moment by the square of purple fabric as it ripples and flags down to the floor. Hazel places a stool at the center of it and beckons Janie to take a seat.

"I'm going to need the donut," says Janie to no one in particular.

"I'll get it." Jeff jumps up, but he is too late. Janie is already up and heading for the other room.

But he is not a bad husband. He will not be a bad dad. All week Jeff has reminded himself of these things.

Janie comes back with a baby-blue inflatable ring that just fits on the seat of the stool. "Don't even ask." She rolls her eyes and sets herself down more slowly than when pregnant.

She sits gingerly, pretending not to notice that T.J.'s shoulders have risen up to his ears and he is biting his lip, horrified. Occasionally, there are moments like this when Janie can see her brother as the boy he still is—body not quite grown into its broad lanky frame, goatee as sparse and well intended as a new urban garden. He is the same small boy standing beside Janie in all the photo albums, at day camp, at the beach, at their mother's funeral. He is looking up and eager to please.

"Are you all right?" he asks.

"I'm okay. Really, I'll be fine."

Hazel massages Janie's scalp and can feel her trying to relax. Janie is breathing deeply, like she is in college on too much caffeine, trying to regain control of her own heart if nothing else.

"Hey," says Hazel. "You should take off that sweater if you don't want it ruined."

Janie's narrow shoulder blades are pushing through her woolen top, which is tight in unexpected places. Janie looks like Janie, but before a fun-house mirror, the proportions off, the curves all wrong.

"Huh?" Janie asks.

"Your sweater?"

"Oh." Janie pulls the sweater over her head and tosses it, just short of the table, to the floor.

And there is everyone, gathered around Janie in her cotton

nursing bra, which is bulky with flaps and hooks and too much fabric. *Whose breasts are those?* They are swollen and wrong— too heavy for Janie's bony, freckled shoulders. Everyone tries not to look at the scruff of skin hanging exhausted around her waist. *To look, or not to look,* thinks Hazel. *Which is more insulting?*

"Here is the body," says Janie. "Can anyone identify this body?" She sits with her arms dangling down by her sides, body motionless, as though uninhabited and left for dead. She is waiting for someone to laugh, to cast out a cheerful line of empathy and reel her back into the group, but no one makes a sound. How did she manage to take all the air out of her very own party?

Finally, Hazel lets out a snort or a chuckle; it is not quite a laugh but it is something. Thank you, Hazel.

"We should probably get this all on film," says Hazel. "So when Otis is a teenager you can throw it back at him: *Pregnancy, labor, and hideous undergarments — this is what I went through for you!*" She squeezes Janie on the shoulder and goes about her work. She begins by parting Janie's hair into quadrants, twisting the sections and clipping them in place.

T.J. tosses his flannel shirt to Janie, and she slips into the sleeves. He takes a new seat on the counter to get a better view of Hazel—he likes the way her moves are quick and precise despite her long fingers, the way the muscle pulses under her bracelet tattoo.

"You know what I think is the worst part about labor?" says Jeff, left at the table alone with the baby. He has not been distracted by Hazel's efficiency. Instead, he is stuck in time—just moments ago—when his wife sat nearly naked and silent on that stool before him. It is all he can see: her small familiar body underneath that extra weight and the set of her jaw that marks her new silence. He can hardly sit still. At night, he gets up to fix the chairs that wobble, the cabinets that stick. "I think the worst affront is that it takes weeks for the baby to even recognize the mother. You go through all that—pregnancy and labor—and it's so long before the mother can get anything back. At the beginning, when the mother needs something positive most, it could be anyone holding him, so long as he's held. I imagine it's awful."

"Thanks, Doctor Spock." Janie brings a hand to her forehead, exasperated, her hospital identification still snug around her wrist.

Is Janie being mean? Hazel wonders. *Janie's being a little mean*—which is okay with Hazel. Jeff is from Louisiana and the mere cadence of his voice can get under her skin, a kowtowing lull, a condescending slowness, as if allowing sufficient time for his brilliance to sink in. Unless that's the just the way Southerners talk. Hazel is undecided on this—no surprise. She is often undecided.

She scoops a handful of Vaseline from the tub and smoothes it along the edges of Janie's hairline to keep dripping dye from staining the skin. She covers Janie's ears and the back of her neck. With her hair pulled back and her skin all glossy, Janie looks prepared for some sort of surgical procedure—which is what Jeff is thinking about, what everyone is thinking about. But Jeff is watching with awe, his wife an island he can't seem to swim to, though he can see her clearly and has made it there before.

Hazel takes up the brush and begins to paint Janie's hair with the mixture.

Janie shields her face with her hands, covering her eyes and blocking out the world. "Oh," she says. "Ah." The mixture will eventually seep in and begin to burn, but right now it's cool and soothing, a mud pack to the scalp. It will bring out Janie's red, then absorb it, leaving only the blank slate of her hair.

"All right," says Hazel. Janie's hair is in a thick and gooey pile on top of her head. Hazel wraps a rope of cotton around the hairline to absorb any drips, a halo fallen to rest atop Janie's ears. Last, Hazel takes a beige plastic grocery bag and puts it over Janie's head, tying the handles at the forehead into a little stub of a bow. "Charming, I know, but it keeps in the heat."

Janie laughs, touching at the bag. She takes the dangling sleeves of T.J.'s shirt and balls the extra fabric in her fists. "I feel so much better," she says. "You have no idea."

"You look sharp too," says T.J.

Here again, Jeff knows that he can't win. Whatever he says, Janie will accuse him of being either saccharine or cruel. He knows Janie—he does know his wife—and so he knows this friction won't last forever. He just hates being the awkward guy in the room.

But as he sits staring at the fog on the windows, the radio starts playing his all-time favorite tune and—once again in his life— Jeff is saved by music. He spent a good chunk of his youth driving to Memphis clubs and digging through his father's old records, and nothing could remind him more of home. "All right!" he says at this invitation to dance. He stands and starts to sway with the baby. "Otis's first twist. Write that one down, T.J."

Jeff squats low with the baby. He twists up and down in a slow spin around the room.

Janie bobs her head along. She likes this idea: Otis's first twist. Jeff responds to her enthusiasm by shimmying across the kitchen, Otis pressed against his T-shirted chest.

"He'll know how to dance, I swear it," Jeff says. "No quick ten-pack of dance classes before his wedding day."

The two spin past the refrigerator and the stove, past the cabinets and the sink, past T.J. sitting up on the counter by the radio. Hazel kicks the purple sheet out of the way so Jeff won't slip. T.J. turns up the volume and laughs.

"That's your baby!" he says to his sister.

Light is pouring in through the windows, and T.J. watches Otis's eyes glimmer as Jeff dances him in and out of every bright spot in the room. All his life, T.J. has spent his time with people older than he is, and he is evermore fearless for it. He has witnessed all the rites of passage before they actually happen to him. Now he sits in his sister's sunny house, beaming, all of life's brilliant promises on display right here in this room.

"C'mon," T.J. jumps down from the counter and slips an arm around Hazel's waist. She has been cleaning up and extra rubber gloves flap around in her hand as he dips her. This is their first dance, T.J. thinks, and it's a good start. He and Hazel will be in this kitchen together again—in every kitchen Janie ever has— and it is more than likely that there will be music.

Janie sits and watches. Look at everyone spinning around the room! There is T.J., delighted, and Hazel relaxing into a lazy sway. There is Jeff, the dancing dad, and Otis with his wrinkly hand held to his face. Here is Janie, surrounded by everyone she loves most—short of her father, the gang's all here. And it isn't that she feels left out, just separate, a soldier-come-home, distracted and far away. How awful it was—Jeff rubbing her nipples to stimulate contractions, the doctor chastising their efforts at natural delivery, the nurse looking so much like her mother, but checking her watch, impatient and ready to go.

She has questions: How do you recover from that much pain? Or more accurately, how do you return from it? How does everyone manage to pack it up neatly and rejoin the party?

Jeff, however, now keyed up with dance, sees Janie's faraway look as a wallflower's smile. He passes Hazel the baby and walks toward his Janie with an outheld hand. "C'mon," Jeff pleads.

"No," Janie says. T.J. and Hazel have both turned to look.

"Dance with me," says Jeff, now down on one knee, the dirty sole of his bare foot facing up into the room.

But Janie does not want to dance. She has all those stitches between her legs and she's still sitting there wearing a plastic bag. Adding insult to injury, there is the plastic bag. She has her arms folded neatly across her chest. "For god's sake Jeff, I'm stitched from ass forward. What do you want from me? Do you really want me to dance?"

This is what Janie says, and everyone stands still. The little radio sounds tinny now, too small to fill the room. T J rubs an eye like he is cleaning sleep away, but he is just watching. He is focused on Janie and nervously jiggling his leg.

Jeff retreats to the fridge, opens it, says, "Sorry," and then closes it again.

"What do you want from me?" He really wants to know. Whatever his sentence is, he just wants to serve it.

"For an hour, baby," says Janie. "Will you just go away?"

T.J. rolls his eyes to the ceiling. He will stand here quietly but he can't watch.

Mean or fair, Hazel wonders. *Is Janie being mean or fair?*

"All right," says Jeff. *He is not a bad husband. He will not be a bad dad.* He absently scratches his neck. "Why don't I go to the store."

"That's good," Janie says softly, without opening her eyes.

The one thing Hazel knows about Janie is that she has an uncanny knack for knowing exactly what she needs: a little potassium; twenty minutes of sleep; a day doing nothing but watching cartoons. Jeff shrugs his shoulders and looks to T.J.

"Sure I'll go. We can take the baby. Field trip with Otis," T.J. offers, though all he wants is to stay with his sister and Hazel right here.

Jeff runs upstairs for long pants and a sweater. He sits on the porch to lace up his shoes. Then they are gone.

"I know I must seem like a total bitch," says Janie. "But really, I can't stand him right now. He's as needy as Otis. I'm sure he'd let me nurse him too. I could have one on each nipple. My personal parasites."

Janie has stretched out again on the window seat and it is taking everything in her to keep her head up, to keep from collapsing into a nap with the plastic bag, the dripping dye, all of it.

Hazel is cleaning things up, moving the stool, folding the sheet. She has always been the naysayer, the stridently single friend oh-so-quick to predict the downfall of any relationship. But after so many years of cynical domestic musings, Hazel isn't enjoying this I-told-you-so. In fact, she'd rather be discussing anything else in the world. The water heater kicks in; there is the dim beat of rope against a flagpole outside. "Look," she says. "At least he's doing well with the baby."

"That's right. He's Mr. Fun, that Jeff. He's Captain Dad."

It should be so easy for Hazel to put forth what Janie's fishing for—something quippy and dark, a wry little smile—but Hazel can't seem to do it. She sneaks a peek at the clock on the stove. If she got in the car right now it would barely be dusk by the time she got home.

Janie drags a finger across the ribbed cushion, back and forth, making the quick zipping sound of a kid in corduroys running away fast. "Of course I'm glad he's good with the baby," she says finally. "He's being great. I realize that."

"Well, what do you want from him anyway?" Hazel says, surprising herself. This is the moment she should be espousing theories on why all marriages are doomed. She is supposed to be delivering her well-worn speech about how people shift like the very plates of the earth and it's only natural to end up somewhere new over time—why lock yourself into anything at all? Hazel has said these things time and again, so why on earth should she feel so pigeonholed! What she wants to say most: *Come on, Janie. The crisis here is legitimate but not permanent, this marriage bumpy but not doomed.* It's the first time she has ever wished that her best friend didn't know her so long and so well.

Janie's scalp has heated up and her eyes have begun to sting. She still has her own questions: How do you return? How do you gather your old self and rejoin the party? "What do I want from Jeff?" She *doesn't* want to talk about labor as a bonding experience. She *doesn't* want him rubbing her feet. "I guess I want him sad and reverent. Six weeks of reverence would probably be good. And I want to be brooding and negative for—I don't know— less than nine months and maybe more than nine days." Janie blots at her face though she knows she's not crying. There's just a single drop of hair dye dripping down her cheek. "I thought, of all people, *you* would understand."

"Do you even love Otis?" Hazel shrugs and keeps her eyes down as she scratches the dye from her fingernails.

"What?"

"I'm serious, do you?"

Janie rolls her eyes, though she knows it's not an accusation. It's just a quick and calm question, not disgraceful but germane. It's just Hazel across the table, Janie reminds herself. There has never been a thing they couldn't talk about. Why should there be now?

"I don't think so. I don't think I love Otis yet," Janie says, trying out the words. They aren't shocking to her, or brutal, only small and true. "I'm not panicking about this; I'm sure I will. I've heard that once the baby starts recognizing you and responding, then you fall in love. And for right now, I'm holding him and feeding him and talking to him as much as I can—I'm not out to screw him up—but do I love him? No, but I'm pretty sure I will."

"I believe you," Hazel says. After all, Janie always knows what she needs.

Hazel is, in fact, rather pleased with this new information. It seems to hold all kinds of possibility—that people can transform; they can start out loveless and end up in love.

——— ===

Janie is in the shower when T.J. and Jeff return. They have bought clams and mussels, lobsters and shrimp. There is chopping to do for a big Louisiana Boil: potatoes and carrots, onions and celery. "Just look at all this," Jeff says, excited to get lost in this elaborate recipe.

Janie emerges in a white robe, her hair wet and combed into a tidy flip. It is blonde without a dash of yellow, white with a hint of sunshine. She is slicked back and sultry, not just any mommy. She is taking silent inventory of the clothes she hasn't worn in months—all the black sweaters, all the baby blues. "This is better," she says.

She does look better, even now, burnt a little pink around the scalp.

Jeff has begun bustling about—peeling carrots and digging around for pots and pans.

Janie is bringing Otis to the porch swing to sit and nurse, and now this. Finally this: T.J. can take Hazel's hand and say, "Let's get out of here for a while. Let's get down to that beach."

——— ===

At the end of the road is the lighthouse at Montauk Point, the black and white tower of it lending structure to the endless sky. There is no one in sight.

"What a scene," Hazel says.

The day's events seem tangled and dense to T.J., but he believes in love—at least he believes that Hazel needs him to believe in love. "I think it'll work out," he says. "It just might take some time."

Hazel nods, though she's surprised at her own peace with Janie's pain. Since when is it okay to sit back and watch your best friend in pain?

She and T.J. hold hands and walk the wooded path from the

pavement to the beach. It's so quiet under the spindly trees, it seems they might be the only people out for miles, but the path lets out onto a busy winter beach. Two pickup trucks are parked by the dunes. They're rigged with trailers, and the sand has been dragged with the bellies of boats. There are two small white sails out on the water and a scattering of surfers waiting for a break.

The lighthouse is surrounded with boulders to ward off beach erosion, and a couple is walking on the dove-colored rocks, slowly, each with a dachshund on a bright red leash. They're stepping carefully over crevices, watching each other's feet.

T.J. and Hazel kiss on the sand and Hazel has a hand in T.J.'s hair, which is so much like Janie's, the same bouncy strands. The beach is cold through their jeans, but the sun is still steady and bright. They lie on their backs looking up to the sky. Hazel has her hair tied back and the big bun of it is making a pillow in the sand. Someone has brought a kite. There is a shiny silver plane.

"Listen." T.J. rolls onto his side. "I want to come back here when we're thirty and forty and sixty. We could get married," he says. "On a beach like this."

"How can you even talk about marriage after a day like today? How can you see that scene in the kitchen and say, 'Yes, let's go. Sign me up'?"

For T.J. this is the scariest question. He wants to tell Hazel what she needs to hear—whatever it will take to force her beyond her own doubts—but she sounds firm and appalled, and he is nervous and unsure. Besides, there is so much noise around him: Hazel's skepticism, the wind and the waves. He can't come up with anything to say. *Just keep going,* he tells himself, *just as long as she never sees him hesitate.* "What are you talking about! What's one bad day when there are all those days ahead! Just think of them."

He pictures Otis grown into a big brother. He pictures Janie and Jeff expecting again. "I'd sign up in a heartbeat for all of it." T.J. is wide-eyed, as if it's obvious, and in that moment he and Hazel both imagine exactly the same thing: a bright day together in a kitchen neither of them has ever seen.

"What am I supposed to do, T.J.? It's absurd. You're my best friend's baby brother." Hazel had hoped to sound cruel, but T.J. is smiling, nodding his head, and urging her on.

"And?"

"And I'll know you for the rest of my life."

"I know," T.J. says. "And it's fantastic."

Hazel sighs. The same arguments run in her mind all the time, and the truth of it is, they're exhausting. She knows she wants something, she just can't say what. She wonders how Janie always manages to know what she needs.

They watch the dog-walking couple out on the jetty. The dog man pulls a camera from a bag and starts metering the light. The dog lady takes clothes from her backpack and starts dressing the dogs. She seats them together, one in a bowtie and top hat, the other in a veil.

"Is this some kind of conspiracy?" asks Hazel. "I think there's some kind of dog wedding going on over there."

"See—everyone's doing it."

Out on the rocks the woman scatters flowers and fusses over the dogs. The man with the camera squats into position. He gives a nod. And the woman—what does she do! Well, she releases a pin and cuts a cord and the tiny veil on the dog is let out, yards and yards of it billowing across the sea.

Hazel watches the fabric lift high in the air. It snaps and twists and catches the wind. It is like a long white carpet rolling out across the sky, either a call of surrender or a call to celebrate. The photographer ducks and squats, approaches and retreats, until the veil blows back and tangles in the rocks. Then the dog couple packs up and heads in.

"Here is my question," says T.J. He is afraid to keep talking, and he is afraid to stop. "Why do you have to look for the reasons to say no all the time? Why do you have to search for every single thing that can go wrong instead of being happy with everything that's going right?"

Hazel looks up. Above is the gleaming belly of the small plane. It is shiny as an oil tanker passing on the highway. It is circling, coming closer to the ground. It would be so typical, Hazel knows, for her to stand up right now, dust herself off, and plod away in big awkward steps through the sand.

"The fact is," T.J. says, "in my gut, I don't see you going anywhere."

"Right now?"

"Right now. And, truth be told, not ever."

With the wind twisting his hair off his face, blowing it up, down, and back, Hazel can see T.J. at every age: what he looked like at twelve and twenty, what he'll look like at eighty and in love. She can see all of it, suddenly, how brave he has been, how patient and loyal and how true.

Hazel sits up like she's about to get moving. "Look," she says, "you know I don't care so much about marriage. I don't care if it's something I do or don't do. And people may shift and change and have certain regrets, but all I know right now is that I'm really very happy here."

"Here?" T.J. is lying on his back. He closes his eyes. *Keep going.*

"With you."

"And?"

She wants to say, *Thank you,* and *I'm sorry,* and *I'm so happy we're both here.* "And I love you," she says, leaning forward, through the wind, toward T.J. and a new, outstanding calm.

In the parking lot, the dachshunds are off their leashes, both belly-down under the hood. The photographer is in his Buick smoking a cigarette. His wife is looking for flip-flops in the backseat. She is going to paint her toenails on the way home.

Just down the road, Janie is folding her sweaters, Otis lying beside her on the bed. Jeff is lifting the lid from the broiler, smelling seafood, pepper, and bay leaves. The steam is rising to his face.

Above the beach, the small plane chugs and tilts, the underbelly catching a ray of sun and zapping it toward Manhattan, toward Jersey, Ohio, California, light rebounding to beat the sunset in the west. The engine spits out a final something and there is a moment of weightless stall. Think of it! That one moment! Where is the time for indecision? Here, on earth, beneath low-flying planes, there are birthdays, and bike rides, feet slipping into shoes. There are people walking a cold February beach and selecting a flat rock to skip across the sea. They are counting the jumps—one, two, three—as many beats as *I love you,* as the small silver plane cocks left and slips from the sky.

The Iowa Short Fiction Award and John Simmons Short Fiction Award Winners

2004
What You've Been Missing,
Janet Desaulniers
*Here Beneath Low-Flying
Planes,* Merrill Feitell

2003
Bring Me Your Saddest Arizona,
Ryan Harty
American Wives, Beth Helms

2002
Her Kind of Want,
Jennifer S. Davis
The Kind of Things Saints Do,
Laura Valeri

2001
*Ticket to Minto: Stories
of India and America,*
Sohrab Homi Fracis
Fire Road, Donald Anderson

2000
Articles of Faith, Elizabeth Oness
Troublemakers, John McNally

1999
House Fires, Nancy Reisman
*Out of the Girls' Room and into
the Night,* Thisbe Nissen

1998
Friendly Fire,
Kathryn Chetkovich

**The River of Lost Voices: Stories
from Guatemala,** Mark Brazaitis

1997
*Thank You for Being Concerned
and Sensitive,* Jim Henry
Within the Lighted City,
Lisa Lenzo

1996
Hints of His Mortality,
David Borofka
Western Electric, Don Zancanella

1995
Listening to Mozart,
Charles Wyatt
*May You Live in Interesting
Times,* Tereze Glück

1994
The Good Doctor,
Susan Onthank Mates
Igloo among Palms,
Rod Val Moore

1993
Happiness, Ann Harleman
Macauley's Thumb,
Lex Williford
Where Love Leaves Us,
Renée Manfredi

1992
My Body to You,
Elizabeth Searle
Imaginary Men, Enid Shomer

1991
The Ant Generator,
Elizabeth Harris
Traps, Sondra Spatt Olsen

1990
A Hole in the Language,
Marly Swick

1989
Lent: The Slow Fast,
Starkey Flythe, Jr.
Line of Fall, Miles Wilson

1988
The Long White,
Sharon Dilworth
The Venus Tree, Michael Pritchett

1987
Fruit of the Month, Abby Frucht
Star Game, Lucia Nevai

1986
Eminent Domain, Dan O'Brien
Resurrectionists, Russell Working

1985
Dancing in the Movies,
Robert Boswell

1984
Old Wives' Tales, Susan M. Dodd

1983
Heart Failure, Ivy Goodman

1982
Shiny Objects, Dianne Benedict

1981
The Phototropic Woman,
Annabel Thomas

1980
Impossible Appetites, James Fetler

1979
Fly Away Home, Mary Hedin

1978
A Nest of Hooks, Lon Otto

1977
The Women in the Mirror,
Pat Carr

1976
The Black Velvet Girl,
C. E. Poverman

1975
*Harry Belten and the
Mendelssohn Violin Concerto,*
Barry Targan

1974
*After the First Death There Is No
Other,* Natalie L. M. Petesch

1973
The Itinerary of Beggars,
H. E. Francis

1972
The Burning and Other Stories,
Jack Cady

1971
*Old Morals, Small Continents,
Darker Times,* Philip F. O'Connor

1970
The Beach Umbrella,
Cyrus Colter